A HERO FOR MAHINA

REINA TORRES

Photographer: Golden Czermak - Furious Fotog

Cover Model: Chase Ketron

PREFACE

Born and raised in Hawai'i, I have had the immense pleasure of discovering life on a tropical island. Far more than a vacation destination, it's been home to generations of my family. I hope to share some of the beautiful parts of Hawai'i with you, and yes, some of the darker side of paradise, using concerns of the kama'āina in my Delta Force Hawai'i series.

I'm making my best effort to be accurate in all things, but like all artistic media, there are times when things need to be fictionalized to make a point. In those moments, please forgive me for smudging the lines and bringing you what I feel is the best story for these characters.

And please know that while some of the locations in this book are actual places in Hawai'i, I'm taking them in my own fictional direction. That's the great thing about writing novels... it is all a part of the fantasy in my head.

Welcome to my slightly fictional Hawai'i!

RESCUING HI'ILANI

Jackson Guard, aka "Ajax," gave up the woman he was falling for because it had been drilled into his head that being in the Delta Force was the greatest sacrifice he'd ever make. Meeting with "Ghost" and "Truck" from a Texas based Delta Force unit opened his eyes. These men... their entire unit were all happy, in love, some with kids. It gave him hope that he could have it all too. He just has to plead his case to the woman whose heart he broke.

Hi`ilani Ahfong was ready to give everything up for love and follow Jackson where ever he was stationed around the world, but he didn't just put the brakes on, he left her on the side of the road wondering where she'd gone wrong. Her manager barely managed to hold onto the 'I told you so' she so richly deserved and helped her focus her energy on performing and building her career. Now, she's back on track.

Everything changes when Hi`ilani walks into the middle of a murder. Fleeing for her life, she runs smack dab into the very man who'd broken her heart. Now the murderers are after her, needing to shut her up, and that's trouble that can hurt the people she loves. Jackson wants to take care of her and keep her safe while the police track down the men. But she's put her trust in Jackson before. She'd given him her heart and soul and he'd left her bleeding.

How can he make her believe that this time he's in for the long haul and not just 'Rescuing Hi`ilani'?

A HERO FOR KU'UIPO

Her dreams kept her in Hawai'i when most of her friends moved to the West Coast to follow theirs. He was on the island of Kaua'i training with the other Deltas in his unit until he fell head over heels for the woman of his dreams.

Ku'uipo Ornellas has been working most of her life. Starting as a professional hula dancer when she was a child, she just resigned from her job as hospitality coordinator for a large chain hotel to revive a hotel from Hawai'i's silver screen past. Hoping to give young residents a practical place to learn their hospitality skills. But someone doesn't want the hotel to reopen and they're willing to take out their frustration on the young woman so dedicated to its success.

Efrain 'Train' Figueroa is a man who loves his movies, but within hours of meeting the young woman with a *sweetheart* of a name, he finds himself drawn into her single-minded goal of getting the hotel up and running. Especially because one of his acting idols filmed on the grounds. When the seamier side of Hawai'i tries to take her dreams away, he's quick to jump in and help. He just can't seem to walk away from the beautiful young woman who calls to a part of his soul that has nothing to do with the ephemeral quality of movies and everything to do with the heart that beats hard and fast in his chest.

There's no script that tells the tale of their love, but who can resist a beautiful heroine, a handsome hero, action, adventure, and love...when 'Train' becomes a Hero for Ku'uipo.

A HERO FOR SUMMER

Summer Maitland loves her job, but as a Forensic Anthropologist working to recover and identify the remains of POWs and MIA soldiers, she can't just talk about her job in casual situations. Some of her family already consider her job ghoulish, it's certainly not something you talk about on a date. Not that she has a lot of free time outside of the lab.

Meeting Kai was a kind of kismet. Or maybe just her friend Elodie's spot on matchmaking. After all, how could she turn down a guy who moved through water like Aquaman and made her burn with a look?

Kai Akina had his share of bumps and scrapes during his life. You didn't swim in Hawaiian waters and not have a few bad moments with coral or the tides. Being shot wasn't something he ever expected to happen and certainly didn't want to try it again. But when he meets Summer Maitland thanks to his good friend Elodie, he quickly realizes that she's everything to him. He'll do anything and everything it takes to protect her and their growing love.

Living on the island of Oahu, the military is an everyday part of life. For Summer and Kai, they're surrounded by it.

Kai's friend Elodie is married to a SEAL and when the Delta Team discovers a body on military property, Summer finds herself with another group of protectors.

When Summer finds herself on a collision path with a serial killer, it will take the combined talents and dedication of everyone in her growing circle of friends to bring her home safely. And into the arms of the man who taught her the best lesson of all, how to save herself.

Kai is A Hero for Summer

A HERO FOR OLENA

Olena Yasui has always been driven to help others and now it's landed her in some hot water. Moved to Narcotics from Homicide she's on the trail of illegal growers in remote areas of Oahu when she finds herself in the right place at the wrong time. Face to face with criminals who have no intention of going back to jail, she's surprised to find she has friends in the strangest places when the Delta Team seems to materialize out of thin air and the one she wants to see the most, steps up right beside her.

Cullen Andrews likes his life just fine. He's the easy going one of the Delta Team. Ready with a quip or a laugh anytime and every time. Well, that was true. Before he met Detective Olena Yasui. Before he realized that there was something to get serious about. The future. Being in a special ops team wasn't easy, but he joined because it was something he could do to help others, and as a part of his team, he's done a lot of good. He just hadn't looked too far ahead in his life, until Olena was right there in front of him. Now he's making plans and he wants her to be a part of them.

Olena struggles with what she needs and what she wants,

confusing the two back and forth as she gets to know Cullen even more. He may seem to have his future planned out for him, but as a woman in the police force there's always a tightrope to walk and falling in love is tough when some men have trouble dating a woman in her line of work. She's just not sure it's the right time.

She has a drive that he admires and a figure that he can't get out of his head. She challenges him in ways that he never expected and given him a dream of what life can be for them both, but Cullen's got two big obstacles to his happy ending: criminals intent on ending her life to end her investigation and her need to protect her heart. He's not sure which one is more dangerous, but Cullen is ready to face them down and be A Hero for Olena.

A HERO FOR SAMIRA

Samira Ioane is the heart of her family. Raising two children on her own wasn't ever her plan, but life happens, and she knows how to lean into the wind and keep moving forward. Now with her youngest in high school, there are new problems she never expected, but instead of facing them alone, she finds herself with an ally and… a friend in another parent at the school.

Commander Anthony Chastain has trained his men well. His Delta Team is top notch and as much of his family as he's ever had. Now, he's taking on the responsibly of raising a teenage boy and struggling with the new responsibilities. Called to the high school to discuss an 'issue' he finds himself seeking the assistance and the company of a widow whose very smile makes him want what some of his Delta's have found: Love, Happiness, and a Future he'd never dreamed could be his.

As their loved ones face ever increasing pressure, Anthony and Samira find themselves struggling to make everything in their lives work and navigate a new romance at the same time. Pressures and stress could easily drive people apart, but maybe the two have come to a time in their lives when they know what really matters in the big scheme of things.

Commander Chastain discovers just how strong Deltas can be on the home front in a brand-new kind of mission to be A Hero for Samira.

A HERO FOR LILINOE

When the pressures of life are trying to smother all traces of hope, having someone to lean on, someone to support you and give you love can make all the difference.

Daniel "Shado" Shimizu has a secret. He's been falling in love and none of his team knows about it. Meeting Lilinoe turned his world upside down, but unlike his other teammates who'd fallen for their women and went blissfully on their way, he's hesitant. Not about love, he's head over heels for the beautiful woman, but she's tied to the Big Island and he's a military man. How would this work?

Lilinoe Keahi knows she's going crazy. With all the stress her family is under, how could she find herself falling for a soldier stationed on Oahu? That was crazy talk. It shouldn't matter that his smile makes her breathless and his kiss? She didn't have time or the energy to fall in love at all. Her family's farm is in jeopardy, and it's going to take a miracle to save it, but Shado makes her feel like miracle's aren't all that impossible to find.

Bad news turns to worse as Lilinoe and her family are

being threatened by men who seem to have all the power and none of the rules apply to them. It's going to come as a shock when those men run up against one pissed off Delta and his friends. Will Shado be A Hero for Lilinoe?

A HERO FOR TEHANI

Fate and cupid can be cruel taskmasters. But they can also be jokesters in their own way.

Devon "Boss" Boseman is the latest addition to Delta Force Hawaii. He knew it was going to be difficult to replace one of the team. Being in Special Forces has been something he's worked for, even before joining the Army. He never expected to join a team that would be mourning one of their closest friends. He has that weight on his shoulders and the push of his family to build a family of his own.

But Devon is the BOSS of his own life. He'll do things on his timetable.

Tehani Teva is a young woman who has worked for a living for as long as she can remember. Having no real family of her own, she strives to make a connection to her culture through her dance. But there is only so much time that she can devote to it because she works for a local airline as a flight attendant.

An unruly and out of control passenger makes what should be a normal flight into a fright and stepping in to help her out of a bind is a devastatingly handsome passenger who shows the handsy man who's the boss in that situation.

Their lives have been thrown together by turbulence in the air, but their attraction soon becomes a love that they didn't expect. And, as things in her professional life take a turn for the worst, Boss will need to step up and show that he's a Hero for Tehani.

A HERO FOR MAHINA

Sometimes the ones who fight the hardest fall in love the fastest.

Everyone knows that Malcom "Baron" Roth is the prickliest member of the team. He's harsh, rude, and sometimes downright ornery. And he's good with that. Protecting yourself is easy when no one gets too close. He's seen all of his teammates, hell, even their commander, fall victim to the fairer sex, But he's not going to fall into that trap. Nope. Not happening.

Mahina Yoshino is a driven woman. She puts everything into her passion. Wildlife. she wants to protect it, even if that means staging her own stake out. Baron's not about to let her go it alone. He'll do what it takes to keep her safe.

She finds out quickly enough that she's not dealing with destructive kids, she's dealing with a criminal element that doesn't like being watched. When they have her on the run, she runs right into a man she's been trying to avoid. The darkly handsome Army soldier who she's seen… everywhere.

There's an evil in the air that surrounds them. A criminal mastermind who seems to be everywhere that the Delta

Team has been in Hawaii. He's taken a special interest in this woman and no one is prepared for what that might cost the Deltas and their ever-growing circle of loved ones.

Baron's beyond the point of protecting himself. He needs to protect Mahina like she's his moon, constantly pulled in her direction. When she's taken from him, he'll move heaven and earth to prove that he's a Hero for Mahina.

ONE

Baron sat in the Chicago Airport listening to the music on the speakers. It wasn't enough to pique his interest. Instead, it droned on and on letting him ruminate about the things that he'd been ignoring just to keep his head on straight.

Still, it didn't change a thing about why he'd gone back to Chicago. He'd gone back to see his father for the last time.

His dad was a raging SOB all of his life. He'd been like a monolith in the path of a hurricane, unmoving even when the world around him was falling apart or imploding.

Raymond Roth didn't have any weaknesses as far as he was concerned. He'd go toe to toe with anyone to prove a point. And he had.

He'd raised his son the same way, telling him time and time again how lucky Baron was that he didn't have a mother to wipe his nose, spoil, or coddle him.

"A man doesn't need a woman for anything if he can cook his own damn meals and wash his own damn clothes."

Baron learned early enough not to mention anything nice that a woman did for him.

On the rare occurrence that he'd been invited to have

dinner at a classmate's house, Baron knew to keep quiet about anything his friend's mother might do for him.

Even in those days, he knew that his father's feelings and actions were wrong, or at least skewed by loss. He didn't dare talk to his father about it again.

Baron lifted his hand up and rubbed his fingers against his cheek.

It was an introspective moment for him. And a moment when he felt the ghost-like sting against his cheek.

His father hadn't made him bleed that day, but he'd gotten his message across.

Comfort, no matter how good the intent, weakened a man. Made them weak, needy, and soft as fuck.

There were times when Baron appreciated or even admired his father's edicts and mindset, but since he'd been a part of Ajax's team, things have changed.

Baron had changed.

So, when he got the call from his father's neighbor saying his dad's health was failing, he balked at first.

His dad had always believed that being sick was a failure.

Needing anything from another person was a failure.

Still, he couldn't ignore that his father was likely reaching the end of this life and Baron did have love for the old man. That's why he'd gone back to his hometown to say goodbye.

He'd arrived just in time to say those words before his father faded away.

The last vestige of a blood relation that Baron had and he didn't know what to feel about being alone in the world, but he knew where he belonged.

He missed the easy rhythm of Hawaiian music and the sound of the ocean rolling over rocks at the water's edge. When they'd first moved to the islands, he'd rolled his eyes at what he felt was a thin veneer of cheerful 'aloha' that they put on for the tourists.

Now, he knew it for what it was, the gentle and unending tide of aloha that had somehow become part of him. Not inside, he reasoned, but it was so often around him that it felt like...

He dropped his head down between his shoulders and he turned his head back and forth in a heavy shake.

... Home.

His phone chirped and he pulled it from his back pocket.

> MRS. AJAX: You okay?

He smiled at the words and knew that his team leader's wife was still on her maternity leave from Honolulu P.I. The hit television show that she'd costarred in almost since he'd met her.

She was likely letting her maternal hormones run away with her.

> B: Keeping tabs on me?

He could imagine her exasperated sigh combined with a roll of her eyes.

> MRS. AJAX: Of course I am. Duh! Besides, Samira has been keeping me informed about your plans because we're going to have a welcome back party for you.

Baron groaned aloud. Loud enough to turn the heads of two women across the aisle who had been talking to each other.

He ignored them like he wanted to be ignored and typed a message back.

> B: Don't waste your time or money. I'd be happy with a beer and a pound of poke from Foodland.

Dots appeared and disappeared over and over and he knew that he'd stepped in it somewhere.

When the message finally came through he read it and felt like hell.

It wasn't from Hi'ilani. It was from her husband. His team leader.

> AJAX: Don't be a fucking ass, Roth. The women have been planning your party and you're going to show up and act like a fucking human. Hi'i doesn't need the stress and you know it.

Baron knew that she was on modified bed rest and he could say it was part of the reason that he'd said what he did, but really he just didn't want a fuss.

> AJAX: When you get your arrival details, let me or the Cmdr know and we'll take care of the rest.

> AJAX: Until then you know what to do

Fuck.

Yeah, he knew.

> B: Hi'i, I'm sorry. I've been stuck in this airport for too long, but that was no excuse for how I talked to you. Thanks for thinking of me, okay?

Then he added a phrase he'd learned over a year ago. A

phrase that he'd memorized from all the times that he'd had to use it.

> B: e kala mai ia'u

Forgive me

He hoped that Hi'ilani would accept his apology. She'd been nothing but kind to him and damn it, he needed to do better.

The Public Announcement System came to life, shouting from the rafters. "To the passengers waiting for flight AG Four Two Five to the Daniel K Inouye International Airport in Hawaii, the flight has been pushed off until tomorrow morning at Seven Thirty in the morning. Repeating. Flight AG Four Two Five will depart tomorrow morning at Seven Thirty."

Baron hung his head and groaned.

As he felt the blood rushing to the top of his head, he heard the ping of an incoming message.

Lifting his phone, he saw that it was from Hi'ilani.

Her message was as simple as she was kind and beautiful.

> MRS. AJAX: Maika'i

Smiling, he sat back in his chair, ready to relax for the next so many hours. She'd told him that it was OK.

He didn't deserve any of his friends or their women.

He was just damn lucky he had them.

SEVERAL WEEKS LATER...

Mahina Yoshino pulled into the driveway of her friend Olena and left the engine running. She put the car in park and set the parking brake because the Yasui home was on the side of a mountain. As lovely as the home was and as well as the property was constructed and maintained, Mahina didn't trust herself.

With her luck, she would get out and her Jeep would roll back down the driveway and crash into a car parked across the street, or a house.

As it was, she was already struggling to hold herself together.

Squeezing her eyes shut, she gripped the sides of the wheel and laid her forehead on the top.

The passenger door opened up and then the car dipped a little toward the passenger side. "Hey, you."

Mahina smiled even though she was on the verge of tears. "Hey."

She didn't have to look to know that it was Olena sitting beside her.

"I came out when I saw your headlights. Don't worry about rushing inside." She sat back on the passenger seat and let out a breath.

"How bad is it this time?"

Mahina pushed back from the steering wheel and leaned her elbow on the window frame while she waited.

"Not too bad. She went to the mall and couldn't find Iida's on the ground floor."

The mall. She meant Ala Moana Shopping Center. And Iida's was a little store that had items from Japan. They carried clothing, utensils, gifts, and more. It was a store that her mother had worked at for years.

Now she was going there every so often as if she was headed to work.

The problem was that she'd retired from work a few years ago.

And Iida's had closed years before that.

"Was it bad?" Mahina wasn't sure she wanted to know.

Olena hesitated, and that alone made her stomach twist.

"If you want, you can probably talk to my dad. He was the one who picked her up from the mall."

Tears pooled on her lashes and Mahina blew out a shaky breath. "I don't know how I'll be able to thank him. Did he say if she owes anyone money? I... I can pay him back and-"

Olena touched her arm and gave it a squeeze. "If there was, you know he wouldn't tell you."

She shook her head. "No. No, I don't want to cost your parents any money. Your dad is already doing too much."

"Look," Olena leveled a look at her that brooked no argument, "come inside. My mom and your mom are having tea and watching *Abarenbo Shogun* on streaming."

That piqued Mahina's interest. "Really? I haven't seen that in ages!"

"So," Olena gave her a wink, "let's go inside and you can see that your mom is okay and when my dad gets home, we'll talk about what we need to do next."

The words she used had tears swimming in her eyes. "We?"

Olena pulled her into her arms. "We've been friends forever. Our moms, too. We're all concerned about what's happening to your mom, and I know I've heard my parents talking about it. We're all interested in making sure that she's getting the care that she needs."

They hugged each other tight for a long moment before Mahina leaned back a little.

"I think we should go inside."

Olena smiled at her. "Ready?"

Mahina shook her head. "No, not really, but I don't think my ribs could handle being squeezed against my stick shift anymore."

They broke apart laughing and got out of Mahina's Jeep.

Later that night, with her mother asleep in the Yasui's guest room, Mahina sat down at the table with Olena and her mother and father.

Her father worked as a Captain for the Honolulu Police Department. He put fear into the hearts of criminals and kept hundreds of police officers in line, but sitting at his dinner table, trying to give her an encouraging smile, he looked like the same man who'd driven his kids to softball practice and coached them too.

He was the same man who bandaged her knees when she fell roller skating and took them all for shave ice afterwards.

He was, quite simply, the only father figure she'd ever had.

"The Security Office at Ala Moana called me when they saw the number on your mother's bracelet."

Mahina nodded. It was a precaution they'd taken when her mother had gone wandering and was missing late into the night.

At first, Mahina had balked at the idea.

Things weren't that bad. They couldn't be.

But she knew in her head what her heart wasn't quite ready to admit. What had been a strange and puzzling problem wasn't getting any better and wasn't going away.

"Was she... upset? Did she cause a scene?"

She saw the look on his face and knew that he was struggling with what he had to say. "She wasn't happy. She kept insisting that the store should be there and that she was starting work in a few minutes." He looked at his wife and she put her hand on his, giving him silent encouragement. "She was starting to struggle when I pulled up in my car. Officer Garza, who got there before me, was a little worried. I could tell he didn't know how to calm her down. And he was hoping that he wouldn't have to restrain her. Your mother is very petite."

"And skinny," Mahina added. "She probably looks like she might break into pieces if someone tried to squeeze her too tight."

Olena's mother, Lynn, smiled at her. "She always had such a delicate bone structure."

Mahina smiled. Her mother had been a real beauty as a young woman. She'd seen so many photos of her in beautiful dresses, beaming at the camera. Pictures at parties and the events surrounding the Cherry Blossom Festival. Her mother had been the Cherry Blossom Queen in her youth.

So many people who knew her mother as a younger woman always remarked that she had been a true beauty, but said nothing after it.

It was as if they were thinking the words 'but not anymore,' but had the manners not to say them.

"Mahina?"

She heard Lynn's voice and lifted her head. "S-sorry, my mind was drifting a little."

"Don't be sorry, sweetheart. None of this is easy." Lynn's heart was in her eyes. This might be hard on Mahina, but it was also hard on Lynn. They'd known each other longer, after all. "It's hard for me to look at her and see her so lost."

"Did," she looked from Lynn back to her husband, "did it last long? Her... confusion?"

Ken, Olena's father, hesitated. "Once I got there, it took just a few minutes for her to settle down. I think it helped that she knew me."

Olena agreed. "She felt comfortable once she knew someone. Something familiar."

"I... I was at work until I got your call. We've been having some issues out at Kaena Point over the last few weeks. I got back as soon as I could without breaking any speed limits." She hedged a smile at both Olena and Ken. "I know too many police to get pulled over for that. I'd never live it down."

Olena leaned against her shoulder. "You're just too careful a driver, you mean. And we had your mom taken care of, so you didn't have to rush."

"I don't want any of you to feel that you have to take care of her."

"None of us feel like we have to, Mahina. Your mother is a part of our family, just like you are." Ken squeezed his wife's hand and they both looked at her. "We're happy to do anything we can for you both."

Mahina looked down at the brochures on the table and the images swam in front of her eyes. "They don't make these with neon lights to flash on and off saying I'M THE ANSWER?"

"I wish it was that easy." Lynn sighed. "There are too many options. We can look at having an in-home care."

Mahina winced at the words. "She doesn't like anyone in our house."

Lynn and Ken shared a look. They understood.

Olena nudged at one of the brochures. "There's a senior day care," her nose wrinkled, "that sounds kind of weird."

Lynn gave her daughter a pointed, wide-eyed look.

And Olena responded with an odd shrug of her shoulders. "Sorry."

Mahina waved it off. "It's not the best name for it, but it might be an option." She pulled the brochure toward her and opened it up. There were a few facilities around town, but nothing close to her work.

She didn't like the idea of being so far from her mother.

If something happened and she needed to come back into town, depending on traffic, it could take nearly an hour or more to get to the nearest center.

Her stomach ached at the thought of her mother waiting for her to get back to the center to calm her down.

Or pick her up.

It was all so much.

"Maybe, if you want to," Lynn's voice was soft, almost hesitant, "we could go with you to look at a few of the assisted living centers near here. They have tours and a chance for your mother to see the facilities and meet some of the residents."

Mahina nodded and switched to a few of the brochures from those assisted living facilities.

She could tell by looking at them that they were expensive.

Of course they would be. These facilities were twenty-four-hour care. They had medical personnel. They had activities and served meals. They had buses that took their residents to shopping centers and medical appointments.

Mahina lifted one flap of the nearest brochure and she almost fainted when she saw the cost.

Per month.

Oh god.

"I think... I... could I take a look at these tonight and then we can talk about which facilities to visit?" She hoped she put on a convincing smile. She needed some time to look at the numbers so she wouldn't burst into tears in front of the Yasui family.

It was hard to think about how this must look to them.

She didn't doubt how much they cared about her and her mom.

They'd known each other for too many years for her to think otherwise. It was a rare thing, she realized, to have friends that were as close as family.

Or for her, it was just rare to have friends. Her mother had always made things like parties or playdates a little bit of a minefield.

And still, here they were, seated around the dinner table,

trying to help her find a way to take care of her mom who was struggling with dementia.

She wished that she could be more help, but she was struggling with not only the diagnosis, but also with the idea that she was losing her mother when she still felt she barely knew her.

The flash of light through the windows shook her out of her thoughts.

A quick look at the clock on the wall told her just how late it was.

"Oh, that's got to be Cullen. He said he was coming home soon."

Mahina shifted on her chair and looked out the window by the front door before she looked at Olena. "I thought I saw his car out in front of your place."

"He got a ride to the base last week. They had a... a training they had to do. They thought it would be a week, but it ended up almost two. And... it looks like he's home!"

With that, Mahina knew that their family discussion was at an end for the day.

Or night, as the case may be.

She got up when Mahina did, but stayed to gather the brochures together. She paused and looked up at Lynn and Ken. "Are you okay if I take these home with me?"

"Please, I got those for you." Lynn's smile always made her feel better. "I have a set here that I'll be looking through again. They were giving them out at the AARP information session."

Mahina put the papers in her bag and moved around to give them both hugs, taking more time with Lynn as she really did give the most amazing hugs. "Thanks. To both of you. I can't tell you how much your help means to me."

Lynn's smile pinched a little at the corners. "I know this isn't easy. It's hard enough for me to see her struggling, but she's your mother. I can't imagine what you're going through."

Mahina gave the side of her bag a pat. "These are a huge help. Thanks."

She headed for the door and stopped just shy of it.

"Mahina?"

She turned to look at Ken. He had his arm around his wife, and the sight gave her a pang of envy. No, envy wasn't the right word, but it was as close as she could get at the moment. They were just so perfect together.

And Ken had always been the most amazing dad to Olena and her brothers.

He didn't withhold his affection from her either, even though she was just the child of his wife's friend.

She didn't think she could ever tell him how much it had meant to her over the years, and especially now.

He looked at her and nodded. "Do you want to stay the night here?"

She started to balk at the idea, but he pressed on. "You could stay in Olena's old room. It would almost be like it was when you were little girls."

Mahina smiled and shook her head. "Thank you, but I really need to get back home tonight. I need a shower and clean clothes. It always feels like I've been rolling around in the dirt instead of walking on it." She looked out the window and saw Olena jump into Cullen's arms. "I'll be back in the morning to pick up my mom and feed her breakfast before I take her home."

"Why don't we keep her here tomorrow," Lynn suggested, "I have a day off and there are some Kurosawa movies we can watch. I was even thinking of making some cone sushi with your mother."

Like one of Pavlov's dogs, Mahina's mouth watered at the suggestion. "That sounds delicious."

"Great." Lynn leaned her head against her husband's shoulder for a moment. "Tomorrow night you come to dinner and we'll have sushi along with the rest of our meal."

"Thank you." She fought back the tears she felt welling on her lashes again. "Thank you both for everything."

She opened the door and stepped outside, dragging in the evening air to fill her lungs.

It was hard to believe that her life was changing so quickly.

And for the worst.

"Mahina!"

TWO

A HERO FOR
MAHINA

MALCOM
ROTH
"BARON"

"Mahina!"

Fuck.

Did Olena have to yell like that?"

"Hey, come on over here!"

Baron managed to hold himself back from adding in his own request. When he'd offered to take Cullen home he knew there was a chance that he might bump into Mahina. She and Olena were old friends and she had talked about how often Mahina stopped by.

Now, he just had to wait and see if she was going to come over to where they were.

"Welcome home, Cullen." Mahina walked over with a wave of her hand. "It's good to see you're home safe."

Cullen, the lucky asshole, gave Mahina a one-armed hug as he held onto Olena. He wanted to tell his friend to get his hands off of Mahina.

But he didn't say a thing.

He wasn't like Cullen.

He wasn't like any of the other members of his team.

Too hard.

Too much like his dad to be around someone like Mahina.

She was sweet and kind. She was fucking smart. A scientist. Too damn good for someone like him.

But that didn't stop him from wanting to wrap his arms around her and pull her tight against him.

"You guys were gone a long time. Olena was wondering when you'd get back."

Baron heard Cullen laughing and he saw Mahina look over at him.

And what did he do in response?

He lifted his chin at her.

Inwardly he groaned. Why didn't he just call her '*Bro?*'

That would've been better.

Olena and Cullen were talking and Mahina was listening to them. And Baron? Well, he didn't have a clue what they were talking about. He was too busy staring at Mahina.

Just because he wasn't fit to have her didn't mean he didn't want her.

Didn't like looking at her.

He certainly didn't have a problem jerking off to those images in his head and he didn't mind the dreams he had of her.

She looked damn good naked on his sheets, and the sounds she made when he was touching her?

SNAP.

"Hey! You asleep on your feet?"

Baron reached out his hand and caught Cullen by the wrist. "Watch it."

Cullen shook his arm and Baron let go of it easy enough. "See? I told you he's exhausted."

Exhausted?

He wanted to pop Cullen in the mouth and show him how exhausted he really was, but before he could grab Cullen, Olena was there.

She grabbed his face and tugged it down just a little bit so she could look in his eyes. "Hmm..." She narrowed her eyes at him. "You do look tired."

He tilted his head so he could talk to her and keep everyone else out of it. "What are you doing?"

"What am I doing?" She grinned at him like she was enjoying herself. "I'm trying to do you a solid. Play. Along."

"You know, my mom and dad have spare bedrooms, since they only have my younger brother at home. You should stay the night."

"Are you kidding me?" He glared at Olena.

She didn't care.

In fact, she was as far from caring as she could be.

Olena poked him in the chest. "What is your problem? You're tired. They have an extra bed. A couple, actually. You stay and get some well-deserved rest and you can drive back to base in the morning."

"I'm going to head out."

Shit.

"Wait." Olena put out her hand to stop Mahina from going. "Don't go yet, okay?"

Mahina touched the side of her purse like she was hiding something in it and didn't want to crush it. "I've got those fliers from your mom. I'm going to go over them later when I get home. So you guys have a great night, okay?"

She turned and headed for her Jeep.

That Jeep was too perfect for her. There was no other way to describe it. Bright sunshine yellow and decorated with a few sunflowers, he smiled before he could stop himself.

"Wow."

He turned and saw Cullen staring at him as if he'd grown a second head or a third eye or something.

"You smile?"

Baron pushed the smile off of his lips and left a snarl in its place. "Asshole."

Olena was already at the Jeep, holding up her hands and, from the looks of it, pleading with her friend to stay.

"She should let her go if she doesn't want to be here." Baron hadn't said it loudly enough for the women to hear, but apparently, Cullen had.

"Let Olena handle it."

"She looks exhausted."

Baron ignored the look on Cullen's face. The look that said he thought Baron might have lost his mind.

"What?" Baron's gaze was fixed on Olena and her friend. "I pay attention. If she doesn't want to be here, Olena shouldn't try so hard to get her to stay."

A silence fell between them and Baron finally turned to look at Cullen.

He'd never seen Cullen so angry.

"Shut up, man. You don't know what's going on. Just... just let 'Lena handle this."

Baron couldn't rustle up a biting comment. That was his usual retort when something was getting on his nerves.

Baron heard Cullen sigh, and the other man leaned in.

"She's got some family stuff going on, okay? She's about to head home to an empty house and 'Lena would rather we keep her here to make sure she's not alone. Is that enough of an explanation for you?"

Okay.

Cullen was one of the most level-headed guys he knew. Hearing that tone of voice coming from him was a shock.

"Yeah." He agreed not just because his friend was upset, but Baron just didn't want Mahina to have to stay if she didn't want to. "Yeah. Sorry. I wasn't... I didn't mean-"

"Okay, she's staying."

Olena walked Mahina over, her arm linked through her friend's.

"When she came over after work, she barely ate anything with all the talking and I know Cullen said you guys didn't stop on your way here from Schofield. So we're going to go inside and cook."

Mahina turned, as much as Olena's arm could allow her, "I'll help."

"No." Olena shook her head. "You will not. You're going to relax and I'll take care of this. It's not going to be Top Chef worthy, but it'll be good. You deserve a few minutes to relax, okay?"

Baron watched Mahina, his eyes fixed on her.

She looked a little nervous, but like every other time he'd seen her, she was gorgeous. But at that moment, she looked... fragile.

And fuck, that rubbed him the wrong way.

If someone caused that look by upsetting her, he had no problem ending them and burying them somewhere in the many valleys and crevices in the mountains.

If someone hurt her physically, he'd hunt them down to the ends of the earth.

Shit, if anyone made her cry-

"Are you staying?"

He shook his head to clear it and saw that both Olena and Mahina were looking at him.

"Me?"

Olena rolled her eyes. "Well, she wasn't asking Cullen. He. Lives. Here."

Cullen laughed, almost silently.

Almost.

"Yeah. I could use some rest before I drive back to Schofield."

Mahina smiled and there was no way that Olena missed

it. She was looking back and forth between the two of them like she was watching tennis.

"Great." Olena let go of Mahina's arm and headed inside her house which was on the same property as her parents'. "Babe, I have some steaks I thawed when you texted me that you were coming home from the base. What do you think?"

Cullen wrapped his arm around her and they headed inside.

Baron cursed under his breath.

"You get the feeling that they left us out here to fend for ourselves?"

He looked at her and felt his face go hot. She was smiling up at him, a little nervous, too. "Yeah. I get that feeling."

"I'm honestly a little surprised," she explained, "with Cullen home after being away for a couple of weeks, I don't know why she was pressing so hard for me to stay."

"Yeah. Me neither. I was pretty sure Cullen was going to throw me back in my Jeep and push it down the hill."

Mahina turned and looked at his Jeep, parked across the property from her own. "It would be shame to dent that. It's a classic, isn't it?"

He smiled. He couldn't help himself. "Yeah, it is."

It shouldn't turn him on that she liked his Jeep Commando, but it fucking did.

She turned her head to look back at her Jeep. "If you want, we can make a run for it. I don't think they'd even notice."

Baron folded his arms across his chest to keep himself from wrapping his arms around her and lifting her up for a kiss.

Yeah, if he kissed her, he'd need her feet dangling off the ground because he didn't want her running away.

Ah, fuck.

He was in trouble.

Running off with Mahina?

Sure. He didn't care where they went. He'd ignore the hell out of the voice in his head telling him that even considering it was crazy.

Spending time with her?

He'd probably embarrass the shit out of himself. He'd say something stupid. She'd think he was some kind of caveman and that would be that, but for the few moments he got with her?

He'd take it.

"So," he bit into his bottom lip for a second before releasing it on an exhale, "your Jeep or mine?"

The door behind them swung open and Baron's back teeth ground together when he heard Olena's voice.

"You two coming in or not?"

Mahina was still looking at him instead of turning to look at her friend. He tried not to read into that. His dick was already hard. Thinking she might actually find him attractive had him throbbing.

"I guess," she let out her breath, too, but she smiled and damn, she was just too damn gorgeous, "we should probably go inside." Her eyelids lowered almost halfway and he heard her inhale.

He did the same and smelled the scent of a thick slab of steak on a grill. "It smells damn good."

"It does, doesn't it?" Her smile made his chest hurt. "I guess we can run away another day."

"Yeah." He nodded, filing away that offer in his head because he knew he was going to want to do just that. "Another day."

WOW.

Mahina didn't know what to say to anyone.

Outside when she was standing there with Baron, she'd just talked and the more she talked, the more she realized that she probably sounded like an idiot.

Around Baron, her brain cells seemed to fall dead asleep or die altogether.

Why? She had no idea.

No, she had an idea.

She just didn't want to admit it.

To herself or anyone else.

He took her breath away.

It wasn't just that he was tall. Olena had a bunch of guys that she knew who were tall, and Mahina herself had known a few tall guys in high school and college. They didn't make her feel like this.

She just didn't want to give 'this' a name.

As a scientist, names matter.

And as strange as it seemed, not giving it a name made more sense for her when the opposite was how she operated her life.

Finding out the names for things made her feel better.

Except in this situation.

"You okay?"

Mahina looked up when she heard the voice and turned to watch Baron step outside onto the balcony and close the sliding door behind him. "I'm sorry. I guess I'm not being all that social."

"Social?" He waved his hand like he was swatting a fly. "Like I care about social. I want to know if you're okay."

She wanted to ask him why he wanted to know.

She wanted to ask him if he understood what it felt like to be seen by a guy like him.

Mahina looked away, over the railing of the balcony and over the sparse lights of the residential area of Nu'uanu and further toward the towers in downtown. The lights always reminded her of the twinkle lights she had on the walls of her dorm room when she finally got a room to herself.

"It's a great view."

"Yeah."

She felt him, rather than saw him, lean onto the railing just an inch or two from her elbow.

"You don't have to answer the question. I don't answer a whole lot of them myself."

Mahina started to turn her head to look at him, but decided it might be a better idea to keep looking out over the city. In the few times that she'd been around Baron, she'd always felt a kind of feral energy from him. And while she knew he was a man and most definitely not a wild animal, she'd had her share of animal interactions during her schooling and work, and the best way to observe a wild animal and learn about them was just to let them be.

There was something inside of her that said Baron wasn't the kind of guy who liked being observed.

Then again, neither did she.

She was more than happy to be on the edges of a room and sit back enjoying the energy around her.

But he'd come outside.

He'd asked her a question.

She could, at the very least, answer it.

It wasn't just polite and maybe a bit social, but she wanted him to keep talking to her, so she had to do... she had to say something.

"I'm better now."

There, that wasn't so tough, was it?

"I bet you think it's a little strange that Olena wanted me to stay when I wanted to go home."

"No," she heard a soft chuckle and smiled at the sound, "it's not strange at all. Olena might lean into her analytical side when she's at work, she still worries about people. She likes to make sure that the people around her are happy."

Smiling, Mahina's chin dropped down almost to her chest. "She's a lot like her mother. Aunty Lynn was always worrying over me and my... She always had me over when Olena and I were growing up. It's how we got to be as close as we are."

"As close as you are? Olena always talks about you like you're best friends."

"Really?" Mahina turned to look at him as she tried to fill her lungs with air.

Now he was looking at her as if he was trying to figure her out. "You don't think so?"

"I don't know. I know she's my best friend, but I guess it's a little strange for me because Olena's always friendly with everyone."

Baron's lips quirked up at the corner. "Not everyone. I've seen her kick ass on the job."

Lifting her hands from the railing, Mahina made a vague gesture. "Well, that goes without saying, but I don't get to see that. I just see how she is around people and I've always just let her take the lead.

"She's always been more comfortable in those kinds of situations than I am."

"That seems... I don't get it." His brow furrowed, pinching over the bridge of his nose.

Mahina gripped the railing again, keeping her hands busy, so she didn't reach out and brush her fingertips across his skin. She wanted to touch him and see if he ran as hot as she thought he would.

"Why? What's so different between the two of you? I don't see it. You're both..."

She saw him hesitate and wondered what he'd been on the verge of saying.

Mahina didn't want the conversation to stall there. She

wanted more. So she tried to answer what she felt was his unspoken question. "When I was a little kid I tried to copy Olena. I tried to have her confidence. To be the kind of girl that people wanted to get to know. That kids wanted to play with.

"I would try to smile more and be... bigger, to be fun. My mom, who was childhood friends with Olena's mom, would always correct me when I got home. Don't attract attention. Don't be loud. Don't run. Don't shout. Don't... just don't. It was better to put my head down and work. Concentrate on being better. Smarter. Self-sufficient."

Somewhere down below, a car honked in the night and it shook her from her memories.

It wasn't a bad thing.

Thinking about those kinds of things made her feel... maudlin. She didn't want to feel sorry for herself. She didn't want to dwell.

"I'm sorry for dumping that on you. I don't usually talk about it. It's better put in the past."

"I'm guessing it's not so much in the past for you."

She drew back, ready to deny it, but he put a hand on her arm and the warmth bled into her skin from his.

"If you want to talk about it," he gave her a lop-sided grin. "Go ahead and talk about it. I'll listen."

She looked at his face and saw the truth of what he said.

Baron might be insanely good looking, but he didn't seem like a liar. He didn't look like he was making fun of her.

And he made it seem so simple.

She could talk and he could listen.

Her heart rattled against her ribs and her head started to hurt.

"*Don't trust a good-looking man.*"

Her mother's warning felt like a window slamming shut between them as she flinched away from him.

Mahina saw him frown again and she wanted to explain, but she didn't think she could make sense of her thoughts for herself, let alone explain them to someone else.

Someone who hadn't been raised in the crazy that she had.

Her mother's warnings were never very far away from her thoughts. It wouldn't take much for them to flare up and make her pull away from something or someone.

Just thinking about stepping over that line had her in a bit of a panic. Wiping her palms on her pants, she took a step back from him, putting her back against the glass sliding door.

"I... I need to go home."

She didn't want to look at him. She didn't want to see the look on his face in response.

Mahina felt like she was more rabbit than human.

Her heart was pounding in her chest like she was hiding from a wolf. The problem was that Baron wasn't the wolf. She was the wolf and the rabbit.

She was doing it all to herself.

Mahina felt behind her and grabbed the handle for the sliding door and opened it just enough that she could step through, backwards. "I'm... I'm sorry."

She slid the door closed behind her and was halfway across the central living area of the house before she heard the door opening behind her.

"Wait."

Nope.

She wasn't going to wait. She was going to run.

Or at least walk like she was in Tokyo trying to keep up with foot traffic.

She made it out the front door and halfway across the drive before she heard Olena's voice and Baron's talking a little louder than either of them should.

When Cullen's voice cut in she was already fitting the key into the car's ignition.

Mahina swallowed, trying to push the lump out of her throat. She'd apologize to Olena and Cullen later. She just couldn't make sense of the thoughts in her head and dark emotions swirling inside of her.

She needed space.

She needed distance.

Then why, she wondered, did she feel like she needed to go back and tell Baron that the whole uncomfortable situation had been her fault? It was the truth, but she just didn't know what good would come of it when it made so much more sense just to stay away from him.

Distance, she decided, was what she needed.

THREE

Making the turn at the far end of Kaena Point Reserve, Baron moved to the front of the group as they ran. He did it easily, as none of them were pushing too hard on the run. They didn't always run full out as he'd seen some of the younger soldiers on base trying to do. That was what you did when you were a young and freshly minted soldier with something to prove.

The more years you got under your belt, you know what you need to do to get the job done. Fast and breakneck speed could be just that.

Putting your head down and running like the wind could plow you into a wall and end your career.

He'd let go of those headstrong ways years ago and did what he needed to do to get the job done and get home, with the rest of his team.

The rest of his team.

Even that was different now.

They'd lost one of their own and it didn't even happen on a mission. They'd lost Mace after he'd retired from the Army to join the Honolulu Police Department. He'd died saving Olena, the woman Cullen had fallen in love with.

And while that had been a terrible blow to the team, Mace's younger brother had moved to Hawaii and later he'd been adopted by Commander Chastain and his wife Samira.

Things happened. Lives changed. And the team just kept moving on.

Baron could feel his heart pounding against his ribs as he ran. It wasn't that he was straining to keep the pace, he could run much faster for longer than it would take them to get back to their cars just outside the reserve.

The fullness he felt wasn't physical at all.

Even his grumpy ass knew it.

What he didn't understand was the ache of it. It had something to do with his emotions, and that was enough of a problem. Emotions sucked.

The problems that emotions created... Challenges? Worries? Searching for the words to express it didn't do a damn bit of good.

You could ask him to list types of armament or list brands of guns and he could go on and on.

Want to hear an exhaustive list of Army battles throughout the major skirmishes and wars since the United States Army was founded?

Well, he was your guy.

Ask him to explain what he was feeling inside, and he didn't have the vocabulary to do it.

He knew that kind of talk would earn him a raised eyebrow and stare from Hi'ilani who had made it something of a mission to see him civilized and tied down like a hobbled horse in a field.

Baron knew that her efforts were going to fail.

The woman could move mountains, that was true.

She was strong in ways that Baron couldn't even fathom.

It was Ajax's own dumb luck that he'd found a woman with enough heart to forgive him when he'd broken her heart and too nice for her own good when she took him back when he came groveling at her feet.

Now she was marshaling the women of the group.

As his teammates fell one by one into the fires of doom and fell in love, Hi'ilani was the one bringing the women together to build what she liked to call their Ohana. Yes, that word existed outside of Disney. Go figure?

He was the last holdout and Olena was probably plotting with her if the other night was anything to go by.

He didn't like his odds with both of them putting their heads together.

The heat rising from the hard packed dirt of the trail felt like it was trying to bake him, and the humidity didn't do a thing to help.

Baron turned his head from left to right and if he'd had a collar on his shirt, he would have tugged at it.

Just the day before he'd seen Mrs. Ajax, and she'd given him 'that look' that said if he didn't get with her program, she was planning to hunt him down like a wildebeest, tag him or do something even more horrible, like setting him up on a blind date.

It wasn't like she'd set him up with someone horrible.

That was the problem.

She'd match him up with someone who was nice and then he'd have to be a complete ass to her.

He could take a woman out and feed her. Maybe even go out and... walk around for a bit. After that? He wasn't the kind of guy to give her a kiss goodnight and drop her off at home.

He wasn't going to go down easy.

And he certainly wasn't planning to settle down. He'd be like those wild cats caught in snares. He'd gnaw his paw-hand off and run. He wasn't that kind of guy no matter what she thought.

If he hadn't been convinced of that before, his short time at home with this dad drove that feeling home, straight through what he had of a heart.

"What's in your head?"

Baron turned to look at Boss as he jogged up alongside of him. "Just thinking."

"Whoa! Careful, Boss." Shado called out from a step or two behind Baron. "Thinking might spark a fire up in that dry brush between Baron's ears. If you get too close, his head might explode all over you."

Boss shook his head, a gesture that Baron only caught out of the corner of his eye. "I bet you're thinking of kicking his ass now, right?"

Baron knew his smiles weren't easy like the others on his Delta Team. The others could make women and some men sigh and swoon with just a quick toothy grin. Baron knew that his face's 'go-to-smiles' looked more Prince of Darkness than Prince Charming.

It was just how he was.

Baron shot a mule-kick behind him.

He didn't connect with Shado, but that wasn't the aim of it.

Laughter erupted from the other Deltas as he heard Shado stumble to the side.

Baron turned back to Boss and shook his head. "Nope. Not thinking about doing it."

"Children," Ajax chided them from the back of the group.

"Awww, dad." "It wasn't me!"

Baron would have smiled at the chorus of childish comments from his team, but he slowed down when he saw the DLNR truck pulled off to the side of the road. A little further down the path, he saw a familiar yellow Jeep Wrangler parked in nearly the same way.

He didn't have to look at the license plate to know that it was hers.

The sunflower decal on the driver's side door was as good as a fingerprint to him.

She was at the wildlife refuge on one of her regular days, but the additional people milling around the site? That wasn't expected.

Something was going on.

Baron came to a stop. The rest of the team came to a stop around him, and Ajax was the first to speak.

"Something wrong, Baron?"

He grumbled an answer, but his gaze was focused on the nesting area looking for her.

"DLNR? That's different."

Baron turned his head toward Train and the other man shrugged. "Just thought I'd comment."

Cullen rolled his eyes. "You know he's already seen the truck."

"And sized up the men hanging around." Boss kicked out his legs, one after the other, to stretch and keep loose. "I bet he's already figured out whose ass he's going to kick if something's wrong."

Shado laughed softly. "Damn, Boss. You keep bringing up asses. Is there something we should know?"

"Who me?" Boss took a swipe at the other man and Shado bounced back and out of striking distance. "You've seen Tehani, right?"

Shado shrugged. "Sure."

They were all familiar with Boss' girlfriend. Another talented dancer in the group and a flight attendant, to boot. She was the latest woman to turn big game hunter and drop one of his team like the prey they were.

Boss' smile and the bright look in his eyes told them all they needed to know about whose ass Devon Boseman was fixated on.

A low whistle turned Baron's head toward the road up ahead. An unmarked HPD SUV was making its way down the dirt road. The rack of lights on the top weren't lit, but with the sunlight surrounding them the red and blue lights were visible.

Cullen met Baron's eyes across the road. "You want me to call Olena?"

Shit.

That was going to waste a lot of time.

Baron took a few long strides forward before he stopped and turned around to look at Ajax.

"You guys go on, I'm going to stay here."

Baron could see by Ajax's expression that their team leader would have preferred being asked if it was okay to stay behind while the others completed their run, especially since Baron was the main reason they'd come out to Kaena Point.

Ajax's jaw tightened into a hard line. "Call if you need us."

Baron shrugged and saw that the casual movement grated on Ajax a bit.

He knew that his team leader kept hoping that Baron's time in the Army would smooth out his rougher edges, but Baron had a feeling it wasn't going to happen ever. He was set in his ways.

And a real asshole.

It would be better to just leave those edges there.

They came in real handy when Baron had to push his weight around.

Cullen was the last to run off, stopping at his side to give him a hard nudge with his elbow. "I'll call Olena. If I get any information, I'll forward it to you."

Baron nodded but didn't say a word.

Cullen ran off to catch up with the rest of the group, but Baron wasn't worried that he'd upset Cullen. They all knew who he was, and his moods were infamous.

Cullen didn't expect him to be any different than he already was.

Movement at the site up ahead drew his interest.

Baron moved closer, stepping up to the edge of the dirt road to peer between the moving bodies, looking for her.

Mahina Yoshino.

He looked for any sign of her ink-dark hair. He wasn't expecting to see it down around her shoulders. At the nesting site, he'd always seen her wearing it up in a ponytail or a smooth bun at the back of her neck.

Yes, he knew it was called a bun. He wasn't a complete Neanderthal.

That, and he'd looked it up online.

Slowing his breaths and narrowing his eyes meant that he was able to save some energy and quiet his body so he could listen for her voice.

MAHINA CROUCHED DOWN by the nest of a Laysan Albatross, pulling on latex gloves and trying not to cry. She'd been told that tears made her look weak and less like a scientist.

She'd found the carcass that morning when she'd reached the nesting site at first light. It wasn't the first at the site within Kaena Point Conservation Area, but it was the most violent.

The KP Conservation Group had been in charge of the area for the better part of three years, and Mahina was one of the newer Wildlife Biologists assigned to the albatross nesting area.

A number of marine biologists monitored the coastline and sea life in the area, but the albatross population was managed by just a few scientists.

Milton Ching, one of the DLNR employees who managed the area, crouched down beside her. "First impressions?"

She pointed at the dirt and dust surrounding the nest and traced an outline in the dust. "Footprints. Boots?"

There was a point in the line of prints where an egg had been crushed and the liquid inside the egg had created clumps in the dirt. Some of the clumps had broken apart and spread along the same line of footprints heading toward the dirt road that the biologists used to access the property. It was away from the nesting area, but when they weren't on the property, a gate was chained closed in an attempt to keep access by the public to foot traffic, but that didn't mean it was foolproof.

And that's what she considered people who had no problem brushing past the large and extremely visible signs that marked the area as a federally protected wildlife refuge.

There were always tracks in the dirt when she visited. ATVs were the new illegal vehicle of choice that she'd seen.

Milton shook his head. "A waste. A complete and pathetic waste of life."

Mahina blinked back more tears and hurriedly swallowed to soothe the rasp of pain in her throat. "I don't know what we can do to stop this! People bring their dogs and let them off the leash. Hikers just walk right through nest and act like it was no big deal."

"Carelessness."

She shook her head and worked to ease the clenched fury in her jaw. "It goes beyond that. I thought it was apathy at first, but this is just... evil."

There was a look that crossed Milton's face, something like ennui.

"As sad as it is to say. You'll get used to people not caring." He stood and stretched out his back, kicking his feet out to shake the dirt he'd picked up. "After you've been doing this for a while, it'll wear you down."

His words grated on her, but she did her best to hide it.

She reasoned that he was trying to help her. He'd been a bit of a mentor to her after she started working at Kaena Point. Milton was a good guy and she knew that he cared about his work... about the animals and nature protected at the reserve. He was just trying to get her to understand what he'd learned over the years.

Milton hadn't said it in so many words, but she felt like he was just trying to remind her that she was new.

She didn't want to be worn down by the job.

She didn't want to lose the pangs of pain and sorrow she felt at the needless loss of life.

As Milton started to walk away, she stood and called after him.

He turned around with a brow raised in question.

"What new steps can we take?"

He turned his head, slanting a look in her direction. "You have your reports to write. Is that what you mean?"

Mahina shook her head. "There has to be more than writing reports." A thought popped up in her head. "I know a detective with HPD. I can ask her."

Milton sputtered a little and the way his brow pinched over his nose told her that he was NOT on board with that suggestion. "You think the Honolulu Police Department is going to... what? Fingerprint the birds? Make casts of the footprints? Put together a line up for the remaining birds?

"Mahina... Miss Yoshino. Really?" He turned and headed back toward his truck on the dirt road. "Really now."

She couldn't be like that. She just couldn't.

No, she didn't expect the HPD to do any of those things.

She was going to take photographs of the boot prints. She had a ruler to lay next to it.

There had been enough of these... incidents that she knew it wasn't isolated.

She knew it wasn't going to stop if they just kept making reports.

It was time to ask for help outside of her job. She just didn't know who to ask.

Olena was her good friend, and she was a detective with HPD. The trouble wasn't if Olena would help. Of course she would. Mahina just didn't know what she could do to help.

Without evidence beyond boot markings that likely matched thousands of hiking boots sold in Hawaii and on the continental US, there really wasn't anything she could do. Still, HPD could stop by and take pictures of the evidence. They'd write up a report.

And she could do that.

She could start a record.

That was something.

Right?

It just felt like it amounted to a whole lot of nothing.

She wanted people to take it seriously.

Sighing, she tried to release some of the impotent rage that was building up inside of her.

Tried and failed.

Pulling off the latex gloves she had on her hands, she walked away from the scene.

Maybe if she put enough distance between herself and the others, she could pull herself together and put things into perspective.

Or at least stop herself from wanting to scream at them to pay attention.

Instead, she walked right into a rock wall.

"Hey."

Okay, so it wasn't a wall.

"What's wrong?"

What's wrong?

She wanted to scream the question back at whoever it was.

Who was she kidding?

She just wanted to scream!

But that wasn't who she was...

Who she was supposed to be.

And she was dangerously close to losing any semblance of caring.

"It's okay, baby. Breathe."

He had his hands on her arms, his hands slowly moving up and down her arms in a gesture that was strangely soothing.

She wasn't all that interested in being touched. Not when she was upset.

Not when she was struggling to hold herself together.

Yet, she didn't shrug off his hands.

Maybe she was just too numb or too overwhelmed to try.

Instead, she looked up to see whose toes she'd quite literally stepped on.

When she did, she felt the breath in her lungs leave in a rush.

"It's you."

FOUR

He didn't know what to think. He certainly didn't know what to say.

He saw the look on her face and felt her shudder.

"Who?"

The question held a sharp edge to it. His whole body was strung tight like a bowstring, ready to unleash its power with an order.

He'd do it, too.

No questions asked.

"Tell me who did this." He eased his hold on her, but he didn't let her go. "And I'll ki-"

"I don't know."

He heard the uncertainty in her voice and saw the searching look in her eyes.

"I don't know who would do this. It's just horrifying. Cruel. And I... I-"

"Fuck."

He pulled her against him, wrapping his arms around her.

He felt her freeze at first and if she started to struggle, he'd let her go.

At least that's what he told himself. He would ease up on how tight he held her, or he'd let her out of his embrace, but he'd be damned if he'd let her go completely.

He could hold her hand.

Hold her hand?

Fuck!

He was starting to lose his ever-lovin-mind!

"Hey!"

Baron could hear the man's voice and knew it was directed at him, but he couldn't seem to care.

"Hey!"

An idiot put his hand on Baron's shoulder and tried to push him back from her.

That idiot was going to have a few fingers broken if he didn't step back.

"Get your hands off of her!"

Another shove and Baron turned toward him, tucking her behind him to keep her safe.

"Just what are you planning to do?" Baron heard the laughter in his own voice. "If she didn't want me to touch her, all she has to do is say so."

"This is a protected animal refuge and-"

"This is my friend, Baron."

He looked down at her and leaned back.

Friend. He'd take that.

"And Baron, this is Milton Ching, one of my coworkers at DLNR."

Milton's face pinched up as he looked between Mahina and Baron. "This is a wildlife refuge, Mahina. What is he doing here?"

She put her hand on his chest and he lowered one arm to his side, keeping the other around her back as she spoke to the other man. "Baron's stationed at Schofield. He and his unit come here to run."

"I don't care if he's in charge of the Pacific Fleet! He doesn't belong here and needs to go!"

"I'm not in the Navy."

"Whatever."

The man was keeping his voice to a hiss instead of yelling. Apparently, he didn't mind trying to bully her, but he didn't want the other people to hear.

That meant he didn't see Baron as a threat in this situation.

He was wrong.

"Well, tell him to go!"

Baron saw that man narrow his eyes as he planted his fists on his hips. He wondered if the asshole knew that he looked like a rooster, all puffed up and indignant.

The other man didn't know that if someone was going to be a big ol' angry cock on the block, it was going to be Baron.

Baron drew himself up to his full height, which meant he had a good half a foot on the asshole.

"I'm staying."

"On top of you thinking this is some kind of organized crime heist, now you have a goon here to what? Twist arms?"

Milton waved a dismissive hand at them. "You better think about this, *Miss* Yoshino. You're the latest hire and you know what happens when the money to a foundation dries up, don't you?"

"Last one in. First one out."

Milton nodded and walked away across the uneven ground.

Baron found himself hoping the man would catch his foot in a hole and break his damn ankle.

It was the next best thing to breaking it for him, and Baron would be more than happy to do it the old-fashioned way.

"You can't look at him like that."

He tipped his chin down to look at Mahina, who still had her hand over his heart. "Can't do what, honey?"

She lowered her hand, but he caught it in his, putting it right back in place.

He was playing with fire, but fuck it, he had aloe in his backyard. Hi'ilani had taught them about that.

Mahina tugged on her hand, trying to pull away, but he didn't let her.

He didn't want to waste any time, so he came right out with the question. "Do you want me to go?"

The tension in her arm relaxed and he pressed on the back of her hand until her palm was flat on his chest.

She had to feel how fast his heart was pounding. He certainly couldn't ignore it.

"I don't like the way he talks to you. I hate the way he looks at you, but I'm not trying to cause you any trouble. If it makes it better for you, I'll go."

He saw the way her shoulders sagged in relief and it hurt.

"Any other day," she leaned in, turning her cheek toward him as her gaze reached across the rocky ground toward the assembled group, "I'd be happy to have you stay, but we had more trouble with vandals."

There was something wrong with her tone. Something that said she wasn't comfortable using the word to describe it.

"I'm trying to convince the bosses in our division at DLNR that it's more than that, but like Milton said, I'm the new one here. I don't think they'll ever take me seriously."

"And having your own fire-breathing dragon around isn't helping."

She almost smiled. "No. Not really."

He nodded. He understood what she was saying, but he didn't like it.

It was obvious that she cared about her job. She was also

putting in an effort, even when she had people pushing her out of the way.

He did that too, but he'd done it out of spite. When he was told no, he did things as if it was a metaphorical middle finger.

Mahina was too damn good for these assholes.

Too damn good for him.

Too bad the angel on his shoulder was only holding on by his fingernails.

He should walk away and keep going, but that wasn't going to happen.

Baron lifted his chin, fixing his eyes on her. "Show me your driver's license."

Mahina drew back from him, her lips pouting in confusion.

"I'm going to leave like you want, baby, but that doesn't mean I'm going to let this go." He lifted his hand from hers and watched as she lowered it down to her side.

She pulled out a wallet clip that looked like the one he used and flared it open.

Mahina took out her ID and held it out to him.

Baron snapped a picture with his cell phone and then dropped it back into his pocket.

"When you're done, no matter when, you go to Lyman Gate at Schofield and show them your ID. Someone will show you to my place."

He could see her mind working through his words and probably a shit ton of cautionary messages, too.

"I know. I'm coming on strong, but that's the kind of man I am, baby. You're just going to have to get used to it."

With that, he smiled at her and took a few steps backward to get back on to the dirt road.

He was about to turn around and start running when she spoke.

"Baron?"

"Yeah?"

Her voice was barely a whisper and as much as he hated to admit it, he disliked this hesitant side of her personality. He wanted to help her break free of it.

He wanted to see her catch fire.

"When you said you come on strong," she drew in a breath and let it out and he swore he could see a blush along her neck, "was that all the time? For everyone?"

He shook his head and gave her smile. "Just you, honey. Just you."

He left her staring after him, wondering what he could do to make sure she came to see him afterwards and not run this time.

WHILE SHE WAITED in line at Lyman Gate, Mahina couldn't decide if she was upset at Baron or just really curious.

It was likely a heavy mix of the two.

After work as she sat in her Jeep, her head leaned back against the seat, she'd called Olena's mother, Lynn, to tell her that she was on her way to pick her mother up.

"Pick up your mother?" Lynn's voice wavered a little. "Now?"

"I'm done with work, so I thought I could come and get my mom and take her home."

"Aren't you going to Schofield?"

Biting into her lip, she shook her head. "Why would you say that?"

"Well, Baron called and said that he was making you dinner."

"He what?"

Lynn was laughing softly, but it wasn't a teasing sound.

She actually sounded happy. "He called here and told me that he was making you dinner at his house on base. And," Mahina could hear her aunt smiling, "he ordered us a meal that they're delivering from Gyotaku."

"Wow." She blew out a breath. "That sounds really nice."

"Oh, it is," a soft laugh reached her ears, "Baron asked her what she wanted to eat and he ordered that."

"Oh," she winced, "that sounds expensive."

"He didn't even hesitate, 'Hina. And now your mother is watching a Korean drama and humming to herself."

"Wow. I... I can't believe it."

"You can't?" Lynn hummed a little herself. "I think you should start driving and get over to Schofield. I can't wait to hear what this is all about when you come home."

Home.

It felt good to hear that from her aunt, but she wasn't quite sure she could just leave her mother there. "Are you sure?"

"Sure that I want you to have a nice night? Of course. Now stop worrying and go to Schofield."

Mahina knew that she wasn't going to change her aunt's mind. That made it a little easier for her.

To say that she'd been curious was an understatement. The way that Baron made her feel when he was near left her breathless some times and flabbergasted at other times.

And she'd hardly spent any time with him at all.

At first, it was just seeing him around with Olena and Cullen and being curious about the man who seemed to like standing alone.

Off to the side.

Watching the action.

That was her usual spot, too. Unless it was just herself and Olena or her mother.

Her mother hated group events. She complained until someone let her leave.

She didn't understand it, but she thought it made sense. Her mother didn't have a filter for the most part. In that way, she was a kind of... a force of nature. She'd spent her life dodging her mother's moods and trying to be as perfect as she could to keep her mother on an even keel. It didn't always work.

So, she should run from Baron, right?

His moods seemed to shift as quickly as her mother's, but there was something... different.

Mahina couldn't quite put her finger on it.

She couldn't quite understand why she was always ready to flinch when her mother was near, but the closer Baron got, the more grounded she felt.

She didn't know how to reconcile her feelings with what she knew about him. The other members of his team certainly thought he was a complete ass. He was crass and didn't seem to care who heard his comments.

Some women were described as having a resting bitch face.

Baron...

She smiled, thinking about him as her car moved up another spot toward the gate.

Baron had a glowering look about him as if he was ready to jump in and crack heads together at a moment's notice. Like anger simmering just under the surface.

And still, he didn't make her feel uneasy.

"Crazy."

"Miss?"

Startled from her thoughts, she sat up in her seat and barely held back a gasp.

Mahina turned her head to the side and saw a man in

uniform looking at her through the driver's side window. "Yes?"

He gestured toward the guard shack and one corner of his mouth curved up. "Pull forward, please."

Oh. My. God. She'd been sitting there with an empty space in front of her. "Sorry."

As carefully as she could, Mahina moved her car forward, not wanting to look like a complete idiot. When she was beside the booth, she put her car in park and tried to collect her thoughts so they didn't think she was brainless.

A guard stepped into the doorway. "Are you visiting someone today, Miss?"

"Yes, sorry." She gave him a wincing smile. "I've never been on base before."

He gave his head a quick shake. "Not a problem, Miss."

Remembering Baron's instructions, she picked up her Driver's License and held it out to him.

The guard looked at her license and nodded. "Miss Yoshino, if you'll pull over into the parking area on the right, I'll have someone direct you to Sergeant Roth's home."

Sergeant.

Another piece of the puzzle.

"Thank you." Shifting her car into gear, she moved into the parking lot waiting area and let out a breath.

"I'm crazy for coming here, right?"

She shook her head.

"Well, I am talking to myself. So there's that." She adjusted her hold on the steering wheel and flexed her knuckles. "If I was in my right mind, I'd go home."

No.

She was lying to herself.

Because she wasn't in her right mind. She was actually considering letting down her guard to Baron.

THE PHONE on his desk rang, signaling the end to his meditation. Sato stood and reached his desk in a few steps and picked it up.

"*Hanasu!*" He felt his back teeth grind together as he waited for the caller to follow instructions and speak.

The man on the other end of the call sputtered out an apology and then launched into his report.

Sato listened carefully, absorbing the information in a rush.

He could feel his heart beating angrily in his chest and rage welling up inside of him.

"She's where?"

Again, the man stumbled over his answer as if he was afraid that Sato might reach through the phone and strangle him on the spot.

That was ridiculous.

He'd find him later if he didn't do a better job and then he'd strangle him on the spot. Somewhere he could dispose of the body without much fuss.

And he'd enjoy it.

"Why," he inquired with the taste of iron on his tongue, "am I just finding out about this now?"

The man on the other end was silent, likely thinking of a good excuse.

As if one existed. "Where is she going on base? Who is she seeing?"

More excuses.

"Tanaka. Listen... Listen to me! You find out what I need to know, or I will find someone who will! How?" He shot back at the other man's hesitant stammer. "How are you supposed to get the information from a military gate? That's up to you, Tanaka.

"I hired you because you came to me and promised that you could find out any information that I needed. I certainly pay you enough, eh? You find out where she is. You find out who she is there to see. And then, only then, do I want you to call."

Sato started to set the phone down, but pulled it back to his ear instead.

"And Tanaka?"

He heard the other man mumble a reply.

"Your future depends on what you bring me. Do you hear me, Tanaka?"

"Yes."

His voice was small, just the way Sato wanted him to feel.

"I hear you."

FIVE

Baron pulled the door open before she had the Jeep in park. He gave a nod to the gate guard that had shown her the way to his house. The guard gave him a knowing nod and a wave as he drove toward the cul-de-sac so he could turn around. Mahina hadn't seen the exchange. She was leaning into her Jeep to retrieve something.

It was a good thing that she was behind the door for a moment. It gave him a chance to get his shit together.

He'd already thought and rethought through what he'd make for dinner a few times and the delivery of groceries to his home also brought some attention from other people on the street.

They might be Army families, but at times they were just as into gossip as everyone else. And the pile of groceries that he'd paid to have brought over from the PX had people talking.

He walked down the path to her Jeep in the driveway and saw the General and her husband next door looking out of their kitchen window at him.

"Nice Jeep," the General mouthed to him before she let go of the curtain and disappeared from the window.

He took hold of the Jeep's door and held it open, trying not to stare at her amazing ass.

"Glad you came."

She jumped and spun around to look at him. "Oh, my god." Her hands touched her cheeks and she shook her head. "I wasn't expecting you to come over to the car."

"I was almost expecting you to head straight home and leave me with no one to share my dinner with."

The look on her face said he was right on the money.

"You called my aunt."

He shrugged, smiling. "Covering my bases. I didn't want you to escape again if I could help it."

"So, you're going to hold me hostage?"

He saw a tentative humor in her expression, but he also heard the slight waver in her voice.

"Hostage? Nope. If you spend any time with me, honey, it'll be because you want to. If you want to go, I won't stop you."

Her gaze darted away toward the ground away from him and damn it, he wanted to kick himself.

"But I'll try to convince you to stay, but if you tell me to back off, I'll do it."

He braced his other arm on the side of her Jeep and boxed her in.

"Too close?"

Baron watched her eyes roam over his chest and settled on his face.

"No," she shook her head. "Not too close."

"Okay." He smiled. "Just keep that in mind. "

Her expression darkened in a moment and he almost looked up into the sky for the cloud that was blocking the light from her face, but it was already twilight and the darkness was inside of her.

He wanted to take that away.

He wanted to bring the light back to her face.

Not that he could explain what he was seeing. Or what he was looking for in her gorgeous face. He just knew that there was something she was struggling with.

He knew that she was hurting inside.

And he wanted to fix it.

He wanted to stop it.

She didn't deserve to hurt like that.

Baron had been all over the world tasked with fixing some of the worst people and situations he'd ever seen or heard of, but he'd never gone into those situations wondering what kind of people they were.

He had a job to do. He had teammates to watch out for.

He did what he was told because lives were on the line, but this was different than that.

She was different.

She made him feel different.

And even though he knew that he couldn't be the kind of man who would make her happy in the long run, he knew he had a chance at the here and now.

It was all he could offer her.

He just hoped that she might think it was good enough. Or at least that it was worth a try.

Smiling at her, he saw the way that her eyes widened at his expression. Yeah, he was some kind of asshole when a smile shocked people like that.

Or maybe she was just wondering if he'd lost his damn mind.

"Come on," he lowered his hand from the frame of the Jeep and gently slid it between the metal panel and her back. "Let's go inside. I hope you're hungry."

She gave him a hesitant smile. "I'm hungry."

"Good." He kept his hand on her lower back, steering her to the side so he could close the door behind her.

The movement brought her against his side and she leaned into him as they walked.

He was glad that she was hungry. He'd cooked like it was one of the guys coming over for a meal. If she didn't have a big appetite, he was going to have a bunch of leftovers and meals for the next few days.

As they made it up onto the porch, Baron knew they had eyes on them from the other houses. He wasn't going to say a thing to Mahina. She didn't need to know about his nosy neighbors.

At least, not at that minute.

But as he opened the door and watched her walk in ahead of him, he smiled.

Let them look.

She was gorgeous and he was damn lucky that she'd agreed to come to dinner.

The rest, he knew, was up to him.

HAVING dinner with Baron was a revelation.

When it came to dinners outside of home, it was usually the Yasui family and they talked enough that she could just sit back, eat, and watch the scene unfold.

At home with her mother, it was a more somber occasion. Even thought Mahina was in her mid-twenties, Suzume Yoshino believed that children should be seen and not heard.

Children were a bother for some reason. Or at least Mahina had felt like one.

That changed around Olena's family, with her mother always finding compliments to offer on Lynn's children.

Mahina had always explained it to herself as something good company did in someone else's home.

Be polite.

Be generous of spirit.

That's what she held onto when her mother-

No.

This wasn't about her.

This was about the man who set down a platter of grilled Japanese eggplant next to the platter of steaks that he'd cooked.

"You... you eat eggplant?"

Mahina wished she could take back the question the instant it came out of her mouth, but Baron didn't seem to mind.

He shrugged and reached for the chair across from her and brought it to the side of the table beside hers. "I've discovered some things since we were assigned here in Hawaii. Things we didn't really have where I grew up."

"And where is that?"

She surprised herself by asking the question, but it surprised her more that he answered.

"On the outskirts of Chicago."

"Wow." She took the platter he handed her and managed to find a smaller piece of steak to put down on her plate. "That sounds so exciting."

"Well, that's one way to put it."

His tone confused her.

"I guess," she hedged, "that it's one of those 'grass is greener' things?"

He smiled and she almost forgot to breathe.

"I guess you can look at it that way. Especially when they dye the river green for St. Patty's day."

She winced. "That sounds kind of gross."

He reached for the tongs and handed them to her for the eggplant. "It is kind of gross, but it's a tradition in Chicago."

"I don't think we turn any water around here into different colors."

"At that time of year it's pretty much the only color around in the concrete jungle. Here in Hawaii you've got color all year 'round. You don't need to dye the water." He shrugged as she picked out a few slices of eggplant, smiling as she did it.

"I've never thought about it like that," she admitted to him, "but it makes sense. I really do love all of the colors here, but I would like to see Chicago some day."

The look he gave her said that he was questioning her sanity.

"What? Chicago is exciting."

Okay, now he really was questioning her sanity. The look he gave her said that better than words.

"So many great films and TV shows were filmed there."

"Like what?"

"Besides the huge Chicago franchise of shows that are there now, I remember seeing reruns of E.R. on television."

"Hmm. I guess."

"And movies..." She picked up a spoon and traced the sauce he'd made over the grilled eggplant on her plate. "There's *The Fugitive*."

He nodded, picking up his steak knife and fork. "That's one."

"Oh?" She leaned toward him, lifting her chin to meet his gaze straight on. "Is this like a challenge?"

A smile spread across his lips and her heart kicked against her ribs.

"Sure," he lifted his cup and took a sip of water, "show me what you know."

"Oh," she ducked her chin down and gave him a look, "*The Relic*."

His forehead furrowed. "Relic?"

"Tom Sizemore. And that actress who plays Heddy on NCIS: Los Angeles. Scary creature eating people at a museum."

He shook his head. "I didn't really peg you for a horror fan."

Her lips pursed. "I have to watch them during the day on a TV, but I'll watch them."

He nodded, watching her closely. "And?"

"And?" Having his eyes on her really was making it hard to think. "Oh, another movie. Uh... *Blink!* With Madeline Stowe and-"

"James Remar. I've seen it."

She turned her head away from him, but she kept her gaze on his face. "Aidan Quinn. James Remar played his partner."

Baron leaned in and bit back what she thought was a smile. "The partner was a nicer guy."

Well, on that, she had to agree, but that wasn't the point. "But she fell for the jerk. He might not have been nice. Or even a good guy, but she fell for him."

Silence fell between them.

Mahina felt her skin get hot and tight.

What had she said?

What line had she crossed?

She dropped her gaze to her lap. "I suck at this."

"What?"

Mahina closed her eyes and tried not to cry. Frustration and confusion tumbled in her middle. "I... for whatever I said to upset you, I'm sorry."

The silence shifted.

She felt it, but she didn't understand it.

"Don't be sorry."

Surprise. That's what she felt.

She didn't know what to make of it.

"Look at me."

Mahina turned her head and then she opened her eyes.

He wasn't angry. He didn't even look upset.

He looked... curious.

"I wasn't upset," he spoke softer than before, "I was surprised. I thought you'd like the nice guy."

"Like him? Sure. He was the better man. He might have even been the better detective, but she loved the jerk." She shrugged. "Can't help what the heart wants."

He kept his gaze on hers as he slowly nodded. "Really? Is that a smart idea?"

"Love is deaf, dumb, blind, and stupid," she swallowed after the litany, feeling like she just over shared, "not that you have to take my word for that."

He turned back to his plate with what she thought was a strange ghost of a smile on his lips. "I'll take your word for it. I've been thinking the same thing since everyone else on my team has gone and fallen. I'm the last one left."

"An endangered species."

She froze after she said it.

She'd just compared him to an animal.

Then he laughed.

His shoulders shook.

"That's one way to put it." He shook his head. "I like the way you think. I like it a lot."

Well, that was a shock.

"So," he leaned an arm on the edge of the table, moving closer to her with a smile, "since you're the expert on endangered species, maybe you can give me advice on how to save myself."

She froze with a piece of steak almost touching her lips.

He wanted to stay single.

That didn't seem like a surprise to her. From what Olena had told her, Baron was a lone wolf and likely to stay that way.

But Mahina hadn't expected the pain she'd feel hearing him confirm that.

Not like I'd be the person to change that, right?

No. Not me.

He'd want someone like Olena. Someone who could give shit as well as he could dish it.

And I, she sighed, *am not that person.*

She lost herself in her thoughts for what felt like a moment, but when her head started processing sounds again, she realized that she'd missed some of the conversation.

"... that's why I didn't understand what crawled up that Milton guy's ass. Olena said you're working for a non-profit that provides manpower to DLNR." He grimaced a little. "I guess I shouldn't say manpower."

"No. No," she stammered, trying to get centered in the exchange, "manpower doesn't bother me."

"Well, don't tell Olena I said it, she'd punch me in the balls."

The bite she'd been about to swallow caught in the back of her throat.

Her eyes widened and she bent her neck forward trying to swallow it down. When that didn't work, she reached for her glass.

"Oh shit. What's-"

"Are you?"

She held up her hand and took a big swig of water that forced the bite down.

When the glass hit the table, she felt Baron's hand on her back.

"You okay?"

Yes, she nodded her head, but inside she felt like a total ass. Not that this was a date or anything like that, but almost choking in front of him?

The last thing she needed to do was look like a total idiot.

"Take another sip of water."

She did what he said, but she also hid her eyes from him. When she set her glass back down, she heard him half-mumble.

"So I shouldn't talk about my balls? That's a bad thing, right?"

She waved him off. "You can talk about whatever you want. It's your house."

"And you're my guest."

She sighed. Guest.

Just great.

SIX

He was batting almost zero.

Fuck!

Telling her he wanted to stay single.

Yeah, it was true, but not exactly dinner conversation.

Then she'd almost choked.

At least he'd steered things back to his original questions about the investigation at the Point.

That helped.

Not only did he get the information he wanted, but getting her to talk about her work changed her whole demeanor.

She went from tentative and quiet to passionate and animated. He'd learned more about Laysan albatrosses than he'd ever wanted to know, but she made them sound fascinating.

The conversation took off from there with Mahina explaining the events that came before she was hired. "They're ground-nesting birds and in Hawaii we have a lot of predators that take advantage of that. After they put up the fence around the refuge in 2011, the birds and plants of that area really started to thrive, but they became a real part of the community. Schools bring their kids, tourists come out to see them. It's just a beautiful example of what happens when humans take their duty to protect nature the way they should.

"And then the attack happened. A bunch of teens broke in and killed fifteen birds and destroyed nearly the same amount of eggs."

She paused then, and he was glad that they'd moved to the couch to talk.

He could put his arm around her, draw her closer.

Mahina was looking at her hands and he could hear the strain in her voice. He remembered seeing news coverage about the event, but that had been a while ago. The news hadn't hit him at all. A crime. Yes, but that was it.

For Mahina, she was feeling the pain like she'd been there. She was struggling to tell the story and he rubbed her upper arm through her shirt, trying to give her some comfort.

"They're dedicated mothers, you know. They lay one egg a year and it takes more than two months to hatch that egg." She drew in a breath and her shoulders rose and fell. "They don't abandon their nest when they have an egg in it. Even when a bird in a nest next to theirs is killed, they will stay. They sit there. They *stay*."

He lifted his hand from the back of the sofa and gently smoothed her hair down the back of her neck and onto her back. "They caught the people who did it."

She nodded and managed a tight smile. "Posting their crimes on social media didn't help, but it also brought attention to the refuge. And while I was interested in working at any site on the island to help protect animals, when the foundation put up the job to work at Kaena Point I jumped at it, emailing my resume moments after I saw it. It felt like I got the job moments later and I've been there ever since. And I love it."

He heard the end of her words soften, felt her muscles tense. He gave her arm a gentle squeeze. "What's happening now? All of those cars at the refuge."

She hesitated and he felt her pull away even though she didn't move an inch.

"You can tell me."

"I can tell you, but I'm not sure I want you to know."

Baron felt the sting of her words like a slap.

They barely knew each other. This was the closest they'd been to each other and the first time they had been able to talk and learn things about each other.

"What are you afraid of? Me?"

"No." She met his eyes straight on. "Not afraid of you finding out what I'm going to do. Afraid you won't understand why I'm going to do them."

"Try me."

He saw her hesitate. He felt like she was on a tightrope, leaning back and forth on one side and then the other, desperately trying to find the middle ground where she could breathe.

He also got the feeling that Mahina didn't have a whole lot of experience with that balance.

Something he could understand.

"I'm going to go to the refuge," she told him while her gaze roamed over his face. "I'm going to go there and find out who is doing this."

He was ready to shrug it off. Of course she was going to find out who was doing this.

He could hear how dedicated she was to her work. That wasn't the issue. There was something going on in that beautiful head.

"I'm going to the refuge and hide there in the dark-"

"No."

"I think I know when and why they do it. I just need to catch them in the act."

"Fuck no."

She sat back, pulling away from him. "I don't think I asked your permission."

"You don't have to ask, honey."

"Good," she smiled.

She looked surprised in a good way. Her face lit up with her smile. Baron knew it wasn't going to last.

"Because it's not going to happen."

"Wait." She gave him a look that reminded him of a startled deer, but not one ready to run, a deer with antlers ready to use them. It was up to him to put a stop to it.

"No." He gave one hard shake of his head. "No fucking way."

She tipped her chin up and glared at him. "I don't recall asking you."

"And like I said, you don't need to, but there's no way in hell that you're going to hide in the dark and wait for these people to come to the refuge. It's too damn dangerous."

"I'm not stupid. I know they're dangerous. That's why I'm just going to record them so I can show my boss that I'm not an idiot or making too much out of this."

"They can set up cameras."

She shook her head. "An expense he's not willing to make. Remember, he thinks I'm making too much of these... these... I don't know what he thinks they are besides a bother. I just think-" She sat back and put a hand against her heart. "No. I *feel* that this is the right way to go to prove that there are people doing this on purpose."

He loved seeing that passion in her. It wasn't just her eyes, it was her whole body. There was probably a different way to say what he was trying to say, but he wasn't used to arguing with a scientist whose heart was bigger than his. Hell, it was probably bigger than the whole damn state.

If he was Ajax or Boss, he'd have the right words to talk to her.

Hell, he was pretty sure any of his team would know how to do this without making her pissed at him, not that he'd say that to anyone on his team. He wasn't about to admit that kind of thing in front of them, or anyone, really.

Baron leaned forward and looked her straight in the eye, wanting her to see the meaning behind his stupid words.

"Babe, you're not going to go-"

"Hey! I told you I don't need permission."

He held up his hand, palm facing her. "I didn't finish."

Her cheeks turned pink and he wondered if she realized that she'd cut him off. He was pretty sure she did.

Baron had a feeling that guy Milton did that to her on the regular. Asshole.

She bit into her bottom lip, worrying it. "Sorry."

"You don't have to apologize to me." He leaned in, his arm over the back of the sofa. "But I'm not letting you go there by yourself."

"I'm not dragging Olena into this."

"No. You're not."

She did a double take, and some of the fire fizzled as her gaze met his. "If not Olena, then who?"

The answer was simple, but he didn't know how she would react to it.

"Baron?"

He felt heat rising through his whole body. She wasn't quiet and retiring anymore. In fact, she was coming at him, pushing back.

That kind of energy rolling off of her in waves had his heart pounding in his chest and his dick hard enough that he had to lean awkwardly away from the back of the sofa to keep himself from cutting off circulation.

She held her hands out, fingers splayed open. "Who?"

Even flustered, she was beautiful, but that fiery look in her eyes?

Breathtaking.

Hell, she even made him think of big words.

He wanted to take her breath away, too.

The corner of his lip lifted. "Me."

"What?"

"Me," he repeated, "I'm not letting you go alone and Olena might get in trouble with the HPD if she did this outside of her job, but even if she went with you, I wouldn't let the two of you go alone."

"Why?"

He shook his head. "Why? Because I think this is dangerous and I'm not letting you go on your own." He continued on before she decided to argue with him, there were better things to do. "If you're bound and determined to do this. I'm going with you. That's all there is to it."

The look on her face... Well, he wasn't sure what it was. He was used to women looking at him in a number of ways.

Not *this* way.

And he liked it.

Everything with Mahina was new.

It was more than like. He fucking loved it.

Mahina's hands moved, her fingers curling in until her hands were fists.

"You look like you're ready to punch me in the face, but if you do, baby, just know that I'm going to defend myself."

"Punch you? Hardly."

She lifted her chin and he smiled. A spark had returned to her eyes and he wanted to see it catch flame.

Mahina looked down at her hands and smiled at what she

saw. When she lifted her gaze to meet his, she shook her head. "Why would I punch someone who's going to help me?"

"You thought I was going to stop you."

"At first," she agreed, "but not anymore. You changed my mind."

"Good," he agreed and hoped that she didn't end up slapping him instead, "because there's something else I wanted to do with you."

Before the words registered on her amazing face, he dropped his arm from the back of the couch and reached out.

Baron grasped her hands in his and pulled her in.

Her eyes widened for a moment in shock, but the moment his mouth crashed into hers, she didn't lose herself in the kiss. She fought him for control.

MAHINA COULDN'T BELIEVE what she was doing.

He was kissing her, and she was kissing him back.

Lips.

Tongue.

Teeth.

So this is what she'd been missing.

He kissed her the way that she'd fantasized she'd be kissed after reading so many romance books. One hand holding the back of her neck, the other roaming over her back, shoulders to... oh, wow. Yes. There.

His hands. She'd seen how big his hands were, but having his hands on her, they felt bigger and stronger than she'd imagined. He had a good hold on her, his strength lifting her against him, fingertips pressing into the back of her thigh.

Baron turned his head just a little bit so that his lips brushed against her cheek. His tongue sweeping against her skin just beneath her ear.

She moaned.

Or sighed.

Can you do both?

"Hold me, 'Hina. Hold my shoulders."

"Sure, sure."

It took her a second or two to remember to move her arms and when she managed to lift them high enough, she tried to find purchase on his shoulders.

They were wide.

Muscled.

He was a mountain of a man and when he put both of his hands on her backside, he lifted her feet clear off the floor.

She felt a moment of shock as she lost the secure feeling of the ground under her feet and then she was anchored again, his body between her thighs.

Mahina felt the stretch of her thighs parting around his hips and a moment later the shock of his body against her sex.

Just that impact alone, as gentle as he'd made it, sent sensations flying toward her fingers and toes only to come rocketing back into the center of her sex.

When she lifted her gaze to his, she saw the question in the darkness of his eyes.

Smiling, she nodded, and his lips claimed hers again. That moment of control she'd had just a breath before was gone.

She struggled to keep a hold of his shoulders when she wanted to touch his face. Touch his chest.

She wanted to feel the corded muscle in his arms under her palms.

She just didn't want to fall.

And maybe he knew it.

His hands squeezing her through the seat of her slacks, he held her tight and secure until she felt the hard jolt of wood under her.

The table.

It was enough to have the solid reassurance of it under her.

She hooked her ankles together just as he leaned her back.

Mahina grabbed a hold of the back of his neck as she opened her mouth under his kiss again. She'd never felt so full as she did at that moment with his tongue caressing her own.

How something could feel so intimate and so carnal at the same time, she didn't understand.

She wanted to keen and cry when she felt his hands move. The last thing she wanted was to lose the physical connection of his touch.

"Easy," he murmured against her lips, "easy, baby. I have you."

Easy? she wanted to hiss at him. How could she ease up when she needed to feel his skin all over hers?

"What was that, baby? You want to feel my skin on yours?"

She blinked up at him, confused.

"You're a talker, you know?" He kissed her lips, hard. "I like it. You can tell me what you want. I'm happy to make it happen."

She wanted to argue with him.

No, of course she hadn't said a thing.

That was all in her head.

But that was before he laid her down on the tabletop and reached his hands up to his shoulders and peeled his shirt off.

When he dropped it from his fingertips, she was stunned. His chest and arms put her dreams to shame. His toned physique looked like a fine art sculpture and his chest, oh yes, she couldn't wait to get her hands on his skin.

His smile was deeper on one side of his mouth, but the heat in his eyes made it impossible for her to care. "You want to put your hands on me, gorgeous? Well, I'm not about to argue with that."

Mahina reached for his chest, but he caught her wrists and held them still between them.

She tugged, trying to free them from his grip, but his hands were too strong. She should be afraid of that.

Of him.

But she couldn't muster up the need to make much of an effort.

There was something delicious about his hands holding her still, his gaze fixed on her. Like a rabbit under the fixed stare of the wolf, she felt a hint of fear, but she wasn't afraid of Baron.

She was afraid of how much she wanted this.

Wanted him.

"Let me help you with your shirt."

"With my-"

He let go of her wrist and his hands tugged the hem of her work shirt from the waistband of her slacks.

Mahina felt it the moment that her shirt lifted off of her stomach.

The light from the far end of the couch didn't quite reach them, but the light above the kitchen sink reached far enough and gave her a good view of his face.

The golden light from the incandescent bulb made his sun tanned skin look like bronze as his fingers grasped the hem of her shirt.

She could feel his eyes on her bare skin, but he seemed in no rush to see more of her skin than what he'd already uncovered.

"Do you have a two piece swimsuit?"

His question seemed as out of place as the strange feel of her lips swollen from his kisses.

"Hina? Swimsuit?"

She shook her head to clear it, but only ended up with her head swimming instead. "No. One piece."

The look on his face was a strange mix of relief and hunger.

"Thank fuck. I wouldn't want to kick some idiot's ass when we go to the beach for staring at this."

This.

Before she could ask what he meant, he leaned over and kissed the inch of skin above her bellybutton. Kissed it and then flicked his tongue over her *piko*.

She felt him chuckle, and the brush of his breath over that tender skin, still wet from his tongue.

"What was that, baby?"

When she didn't know what to answer, he repeated the word and kissed her where his tongue had been just seconds before.

"Piko," she groaned in the back of her throat. "Bellybutton."

"Love this cultural exchange we have going." She heard his humor clearly in the tone of his voice. "I can't wait to *exchange* a few more things."

Before she could put a word or two together to speak, he had his mouth over her belly once again, his tongue dancing over the swell of her body just below her bellybutton. "I love the way you taste. Sea salt." He dragged his tongue over her skin again. "Wind."

She couldn't help it. His words got under her skin.

His eyes met hers over her belly and between her breasts.

"You."

As he kissed and tongued his way up from her bellybutton, he lifted more and more of her shirt until his face was hidden behind the hem of her shirt.

"Ba-Baron."

Her voice stuttered when she felt his skin glancing over the surface of her skin.

"Let's get his off you."

She busied her hands with the feel of his warm skin under her fingertips as his fingers pushed her shirt buttons free of the buttonholes on the opposite side. Inch by inch, she saw the sculpted planes of his face and the way his lips caressed her skin.

When he reached the last button and pulled it free, he opened the halves of her shirt and cursed under his breath. "Fuck me."

She smiled, even though her body was trembling under and against him.

"Do you always wear these under your uniform?"

She closed her eyes, trying to hide them from his searching gaze. "Not every day."

Mahina dropped her gaze to her chest and saw his lips inches from the flesh-colored bralette covered and banded with lace just beneath the edge, across her ribs.

"Its comfortable, but it makes me feel feminine, too."

"No doubt about that." He shook his head and the motion brushed his cheek against her nipple.

She arched her back from the table, bringing her in contact with him again, but this time, Baron turned his head and captured the tip of her breast in his mouth.

A rush of heat and shivering sensations shot through her body, and her hands reached for his head to hold him there. She hadn't felt that kind of electricity arcing through her body before, but she knew she wanted more of it.

The half-lit room looked like it was filled with hundreds of candles.

"Yes." The friction of the fabric against her skin, drawn and teased by this tongue, could very well send her over the edge if she didn't find a way to make him stop.

But stopping him was the last thing she wanted to do.

If he kept up what he was doing, it might only take a few more minutes to-

The phone on the counter rang, shattering the bubble around them.

And before her mind could understand what was going on, the cell phone that Baron had placed on the coffee table rang and jumped toward the edge of the wood.

Mahina had no idea what was going on, but Baron did.

He smacked his palm on the table close to his hip and stood up.

"I don't know how to say this, 'Hina, but-"

The pieces fell into place like the blade of a guillotine, severing the building passion between them.

"You have to go."

She'd heard it before. She'd even seen Cullen all but leap up from the dinner table and barely have the time to kiss Olena before he was out the door.

She knew she was right by the look on his face.

Half regret and something she couldn't even begin to name.

"Go," she told him. "I'll figure out how to close up the house."

His cell buzzed with a higher-pitched chime and he lifted it up to look at the screen.

"Our commander's wife is coming over. She'll help you get off base."

"Yeah," Mahina nodded, feeling a little off-kilter by the sudden rush of emotions and hormones coursing through her veins. "Go. I'll be okay."

Baron reached down and snatched up his shirt from the

chair cushion and was almost at the door before he turned around to look at her.

He came back for just a second, his hand and hip pushing the table out of the way so he could grasp the nape of her neck with his free hand and pull her into a hard kiss.

And then he was gone.

SEVEN

Three weeks had passed since Baron and the others on his team had been called away.

Three weeks felt like a lifetime, especially when she felt like she was missing a piece of the puzzle. Talking to Olena didn't make things better. Whenever she asked for information about where Baron's unit was she got the same dodgy answer.

They were deployed somewhere.

Deployed.

Okay. While Mahina didn't know much about the army or any of the military branches, she had the internet.

Deployments were usually months long, maybe even a year or more! She'd seen videos of people going to see their spouses and loved ones off on their deployments. There were bands and parades, not a quick phone message, and the guys disappearing for weeks at a time.

Unless the videos and internet sleuthing she had done were just all wrong.

And considering that her best friend, who had to know

what was going on, wasn't telling her anything beyond saying, "They're deployed somewhere."

Okay, so if that was the truth, then they'd have some way to know when they might be coming home.

Nope.

When Olena had invited her over to spend time with the other women, she'd gone at first. She'd met them all before and while she was still a little star struck when Hi'ilani Guard was around, the other women were all pretty easy going.

Easy to talk to.

Fun even.

But spending time with them, Mahina was sure of one thing about the unit that Baron was in.

She was sure that she was the only one in the room who was missing a very important piece of the puzzle.

And because of that, she found excuses to stay away from the ladies' nights they had and the Saturday outings.

When they asked her why, she could easily say that she was dealing with her mother's health, because she was.

Since Baron had run out of his house that day, it seemed like her mother's health wasn't just taking a turn for the worse. It was going down a massive slide.

Sitting down in a comfy chair at the far side of the room, she watched as a gerontologist and a home care nurse conferred with each other at her mother's side.

She could hear the conversation, or rather, she could hear parts of it.

"Now, Missus Yoshino-"

"Miss," her mother smiled and her eyes twinkled in the light of the overhead fixture. "I'm not married."

Mahina bit into her bottom lip to keep silent as her mother flirted with a doctor who was probably just a few years older than her daughter and, if the ring on his finger was any indication, he was happily married.

But her mother was batting her eyelashes at him and it looked like she was flirting behind a fan, but her hand was empty.

Keeping herself from groaning and hiding her face behind her hands was hard enough.

The doctor continued. "Your daughter-"

"Daughter?" She laughed, her head tipping back as her bell-like laughter rang off the ceiling of the bedroom. "Don't tease, doctor. I'm too young to have a daughter and,' she leaned in and stage-whispered behind her hand, "not married. How can I have a child?"

Mahina blew out a breath and prayed that the doctor would remember what she'd explained to him outside before he'd come in for the in-home visit. She'd even worn a scrub top she'd bought from a lady on Etsy with bright pink cherry blossoms on it. Flowers that her mother loved.

And a color that Mahina didn't wear at all.

So when her mother was struggling, she'd wear the scrub top

"Oh, yes." He cleared his throat. "Your nurse said that you haven't been taking your medicine."

"Lies!" She shook her head and then waved her hand at the doctor. "Don't listen to her. She's hardly worth the money I pay her."

Mahina's eyes widened and she hung her head. Sometimes her mother would complain to her about... well, her.

"I take my medication." She gestured at the rolling table with the wall of medication bottles lined up along the edge. "Go ahead! Go ahead! Count the pills, you'll see!"

Mahina felt a muscle in her jaw twinge at her mother's words.

She'd counted her mother's pills. And she was right on the number, but there was a morning a few days before when Mahina had picked up the trash bag from the kitchen to take it outside only to hear the unmistakable sound of pills rolling around in the bottom of the bag.

That's why she'd called the in-home office of her mother's provider team and asked for a check-up at the house.

She had no idea how long her mother's pill hiding had been going on. She could have dropped it into the disposal in the sink. She could have dropped it into the toilet or down the drain in the tub.

The doctor was still talking to her mother. "You really do need to take those medications, Missus- Miss Yoshino."

Again, her mother waved off the doctor's words. "I take them."

"Yes, well. Please keep in mind that we've prescribed them for you for your health."

"I think you'll agree that I'm in great health." She beamed at the doctor. "I don't even know why you came to my home."

"With our favorite patients," the doctor's voice was brighter than it usually was, laying it on thick, "we like to stop in and see them sometimes. And because we want to make sure you're in the best possible health, we would really like you to come into the clinic and have a blood draw."

Mahina squeezed her eyes shut. The doctor had stepped in it now.

"I don't need a blood draw." Her mother turned her back on the doctor and lifted her chin in the air.

Mahina was used to that posture. It meant that her mother was done. Not just with listening. She was done for the day.

The doctor and the care nurse shared a look before the doctor walked across the room to Mahina. "Thank you for contacting us."

"Of course. When I discovered the pills in the trash bag I had no way of knowing how many she'd taken."

He nodded. "Or how few."

"Show the man out."

Mahina felt tears prick against the backs of her eyes. She didn't know why, they were just there.

"Why don't you walk me out to my car and we can talk."

"Sure, sure." Mahina managed to get up and out of the comfy chair and walked toward the door with the doctor.

"Don't you two plot amongst yourselves!"

While her steps faltered, the doctor kept walking and didn't stop until he was standing beside his car.

He didn't even meet her eyes when he talked.

"The blood test will give us a good idea of how many pills she's had recently."

She nodded. "How can we make sure this doesn't happen again? She gets mad at me if I want to watch her take them or if I stand anywhere nearby."

He shook his head. "Well, you have to be careful. You're not medical personnel."

"No," she sighed, "I am not."

"You can't force her to take her medication."

A soft laugh escaped her lips. "I'm sorry, I'm not trying to laugh. I just... I remember my mom making me take my medication when I was a kid. It's just... It's so hard to do this when she's so... so crafty. I'm guessing she's pretending to take the pills but then... I don't know, dropping them into the trash can when I'm not looking?"

"You have a caregiver in the house today."

She nodded. "We can't afford help more than a couple of days a week. My mom's best friend watches her a couple of days too. I have some flexibility in my work schedule so only have to work four days a week.

"The days that I'm home, it's like a fight all the time."

She felt her face go cold and lifted her gaze to meet the doctor's.

"I'm not saying that we physically fight or anything."

His easy smile and nod didn't really help the ache in her chest.

On bad days, her mom had threatened to call the police on her for asking her to take her medication or get in the car to go and see a doctor. Sometimes saying that she would accuse Mahina of abuse if she wasn't excused from her medical appointments.

"I'm not worried about her safety in your care."

"I just don't think I'm doing a good enough job of taking care of her. We've been looking at assisted living options," her chest tightened and she lowered her gaze from the doctor's, "I'm having trouble figuring out how we're going to afford it."

She tried to let out the breath in her lungs, but it seemed caught.

Saying the words out loud didn't make it easier to breathe.

In fact, it made her feel even worse.

Mahina folded her arms across her chest, needing the sensation to hold herself together.

The doctor cleared his throat and Mahina looked up.

"I know you're doing your best to care for her, Mahina. It can't be easy. You're a young woman, you should be enjoying your life-"

"It's not about that." She bristled at his words. "I don't care about things like that. I care that she's not taking her medication. I care that she won't listen to me and take them. I'm... I'm doing what I can, but I'm just struggling with the feeling that she might get sick or that her... condition might get worse because she's not getting the care she should."

Mahina's thoughts were running wild. When she was in high school her mother used to drone on about how dangerous boys were. And she'd harp on babies and how it wasn't fun to take care of them. Her words always sounded so harsh, but Mahina tried to believe that she was just worried. Worried that she might do something stupid and wouldn't be ready to have a baby or care for it.

Here she was, barely able to take care of her mother's basic needs.

Her mother was likely more right than Mahina had given her credit for.

"I understand your concerns, Mahina. It happens more than people realize. Money doesn't grow on trees, at least that's what my parents told me all of my life."

She smiled when he did, remembering that idiom coming from her mother as well.

"I'm not saying it's a guarantee, but I might know of some organizations that might be able to help with the cost of a care facility."

Care facility.

What was it about the words that made her cringe inside?

Likely just her guilt sneaking up on her from another direction.

"Would you like me to ask around?"

Mahina shook herself and an actual smile lifted the corners of her mouth. "That... that would be wonderful! I don't know how to thank you for even thinking about it."

She stepped closer and put out her hand to shake his.

"Thank you. Thank you so much."

He let go of her hand and stepped back. "Nothing, really. I just know a few people that I can call. I can't guarantee anything," he reminded her, "but we can try."

"No. No. I'm not expecting anything. Really, just the thought that we could get some help... It means a lot for you to offer. Thank you."

The doctor left and then the care nurse left on his heels.

Mahina went back inside and closed the door.

She looked across the room at her mother, who was

sitting down in her favorite chair, her gaze fixed outside the window.

It was almost too good to be true.

For days and days she'd been worrying about where they could find the money to take care of her mother. She'd even gone so far as to ask a real estate agent how much they could get for the house.

Mahina knew she could find an apartment to live in. She didn't care if it was a box with no windows, if she could be sure her mother was taken care of, but the agent she'd spoken to had let her in on a secret that her mother hadn't told her.

Her mother had taken out a mortgage on the house in the last few years. Something she hadn't shared with Mahina at all. With the real estate market and the bank loan, the house was currently 'upside down' and she'd likely have to pay for someone to buy it, which entirely defeated the purpose of selling.

But that just added to her worries.

Without the house to help pay for a care facility of any kind, Mahina was falling into a depression.

She longed to talk about things with someone, but it was nearly impossible to be around Olena at the moment.

Even when they avoided the conversation of where Cullen and the others were, Mahina felt like Olena was holding something else back.

Something really important.

And Mahina didn't know what to do with that feeling.

Mahina hadn't held back from her friend when Baron left his house like the world was falling down around his ears. Mahina told Olena some of what happened at Baron's house. Enough for her friend to know that they'd crossed some kind of line from mere acquaintances to something much more personal than that.

Sure, she hadn't told her friend all of the details, but she knew. Olena knew how much it took for her to drop her walls enough to talk to a man she didn't really know outside of work.

So holding back... whatever she was holding back... just made things more awkward between them.

And that meant that Mahina felt even more alone than she normally did.

"Are you going to stand there all night?"

Mahina swallowed the aching knot in her throat and tried to muster up a smile for her mother. "Sorry. I was just thinking."

"Thinking?" Her mother huffed and Mahina looked up and caught her mother's withering gaze in the reflection of the window pane. "About those animals?"

"No," she shook her head, "I'm not thinking about work, Mama. I was thinking about-"

Her mother made some kind of disgusted sigh and folded her hands in her lap. "You should let Olena do the thinking. She's such a smart young woman. Beautiful, too. Life would have been so much easier if you were like her. If she was my daughter, I could have entered her into the Cherry Blossom pageant and she would have won! You were always too quiet for things like that." She sighed. "You were always too shy. Too... simple for something that important, you know. I bet Lynn's looking forward to grandchildren."

She knew she should keep her mouth shut, but her mother's caustic comments dug in like a splinter under her fingernail.

"What about you, Mama. Don't you want grandchildren, too?"

Her mother closed her eyes. Mahina could see that in the reflection too. "You can't even take care of me, a grown adult.

If you can't do something this simple," she chided her, "how will you take care of a poor defenseless baby?"

Poor defenseless baby.

That cut deep. Even though Mahina knew that she wasn't in any position to have a child in the near future, just hearing her mother's words hurt like hell.

Even knowing that her mother's dementia made her fly off the handle at times and listless and morose at others, it made Mahina ache inside that she couldn't manage to make her mother happy even if it was just the idea of having children in the future,

Her mother didn't believe in her at all.

Blinking back tears, Mahina ducked into the bathroom and closed the door behind her. Pulling her phone out from her pocket she looked at the notifications screen.

No new messages.

For a moment, she thought about leaving another message for Baron. Just a short and to-the-point text saying that she hoped he was okay, but she'd done something similar half a dozen times.

There was no use in making herself look even more stupid than she already did.

Dropping her phone back into her pocket, she turned on the sink and washed her hands, just so her mother didn't think she was just hiding in the bathroom.

Before she opened the door, Mahina closed her eyes and prayed that the guys would come home soon and safe.

Yeah.

She really was that pitiful.

SATO WAS outside in the pool when he heard his phone ring. Swimming to the edge of the pool, he picked up the phone and saw the name of the caller on the screen.

"Nani?"

There was silence on the other end of the phone. Why? He didn't know. He'd already barked at the man, asking him 'What?'

Why was he waiting?

"My apologies, Sato-san. You asked me to call about Suzume Yoshino if something needed to be addressed."

Sato stood there at the edge of the pool, glaring out at the horizon line.

Waiting.

The man coughed and cleared his throat. "I spoke to her daughter today-"

"You spoke to m- Mahina? What did she say?"

When the man didn't immediately answer him, Sato bit out a curse into the receiver of the phone.

"What did she say?"

"It was about Suzume's health. She may need care that they can not pay for."

"Get to the point!" Sato bit out the words into the relative quiet of his backyard. "What do you have to tell me?"

"Soon Suzume may require care around the clock. Her daughter is doing what she can to care for her mother, but the progression of the disease is quicker than I expected." The man's words stilled at that point.

Sato didn't want to wait for more information, and he certainly didn't want to ask for it.

"What do you need?"

The doctor stammered a little. "It's not what I need, sir. She needs someone to help her figure out how she could afford the kind of around-the-clock care that her mother will soon need. I offered to find an organization who might be willing to help pay the cost for Suzume to enter into a care facility able to take care of her needs. And you, Sato-san. You have every reason to go and speak to Mahina. You can-"

"Yes. Yes..." Sato cut off the other man again. He didn't need the man to spell out his meaning. "I can speak to my daughter.

"Finally."

EIGHT

Baron grit his teeth as the transport plane hit the tarmac like it had a personal vendetta against it. Beside him, Boss hissed out a breath and gripped the seat.

"We got a cross wind or something?"

Baron shook his head. "No clue. I'm just glad to get back home."

As they taxied to the hangar, Ajax got up from his seat and made his way to the front of the cargo area. Leaning his back against the wall, he looked at the group and offered them a wan smile.

"Good to be back in Hawaii. Glad we're all here to not tell the tale."

Baron caught sight of Shado across the aisle. The one amongst them who laughed the easiest, he sat in his chair with his eyes closed as if he was asleep, but he wasn't.

To anyone who didn't know Shado, or the hell that they'd been in during the last few weeks, they would think he was relaxed. A closer look would show that he had was holding his right wrist with his left hand, holding it in place.

And that placid look on his face in the half-light of the transport plane's interior was easy to mistake.

There were lines etched in his forehead from the pain that he was struggling with. Even with the pain meds that he'd taken about an hour before landing hadn't blocked the pain.

He'd planned his medication schedule so that by the time Lilinoe met them at the hangar he'd be able to grin and bear it instead of just bearing it.

Turning toward the window, Baron saw the bright afternoon sun baking the tarmac and every stone surface for miles.

He already knew what would happen as soon as the doors opened.

They'd get Shado out of the transport and with his wife at his side they'd transport him to Tripler Hospital. The big pink landmark on the hilltop in Moanalua was unmistakable.

Nearly the same color as the Royal Hawaiian Hotel in Waikiki, it had been there since the early 1900s and could be seen from miles around. Shado would get great care there and they'd be over to see him as soon as they got some rest.

Ajax looked at the group almost as if he was counting heads to make sure that he still had all of them together. "Unless something pops up, we'll have the rest of the week to decompress and spend time with our loved ones."

Baron turned his gaze back to the window because the last thing he wanted to see were well-meaning looks from his team. The 'maybe I should invite his sorry single ass over one night' looks.

It wasn't lost on Baron that he was the last free-range Delta of the group.

He didn't need anyone to invite him over, he had plenty to keep him busy.

Besides, the last thing he wanted to be was the extra

wheel wobbling around when they'd just gotten back from a mission.

Across the aisle, Cullen leaned forward and gave him a look. "You, uh... going to come over to my place for dinner tonight? Tomorrow?"

Boss barely smothered a laugh at the end of Cullen's question and Baron barely resisted shoving the man out of his chair and onto the floor.

When Baron opened his mouth to tell Cullen he was fine on his own, the words that came out weren't what he expected at all.

"I've got to talk to Mahina, first."

Train turned around on his seat and looked at Baron, shock clearly written on his face. "Mahina?"

Cullen answered Train's question. "Mahina, Olena's friend."

Train and Ajax shared a look. There was no way that Hi'ilani wasn't going to hear about this.

Blowing out a breath, he glared at an invisible spot on the wall behind Ajax, but whoever said 'No rest for the wicked,' certainly knew what they were talking about when Cullen spoke again. "You know what you're going to say?"

Baron turned and he was fairly sure that his glare told Cullen to back-the-fuck-off, but since when did the other guys on his team actually leave him alone?

Ajax sat down and leaned his forearms on his knees. "What's going on?"

What's going on?

What Ajax should be asking was 'What went on?'

But that wasn't any of his damn business.

Ajax wasn't about to let it go. "You know there are certain things you can't tell her."

"Unless," Cullen shifted on his chair, "you've got a lot to tell us."

Baron's head swiveled around until he glared at Cullen. "I doubt Olena would be okay with you asking questions like that about her best friend."

Beside him, Boss lifted a brow at his words. "The ladies would say that your Freudian slip is showing, man. Your mind went-"

Baron turned his hand and extended his middle finger at the group as a whole. "Fuck Freud. And the rest of you can calm the fuck down."

"Baron." From the shadows came the cautionary tone of Anthony Chastain, the commander who watched out for their collective asses. "Watch your language."

Baron wanted to tell them all where to step off, but he knew what they were talking about. "I haven't said a thing to her about what we do. It's not like we've talked about what I do."

Boss's expression changed into almost a smirk and even Shado opened his eyes to look at Baron.

"Now I want to know what you two have been doing." Shado groaned and his eyelids closed as the plane came to a final stop.

The team got up, with the exception of Shado and they made sure that the way was clear so that they could get a wheelchair through the aisle to transport Shado to an ambulance for his move to Tripler Hospital.

The commander went with Shado to the ambulance and to make sure that Lilinoe was able to see her husband.

The rest of the team waited for the ground crew to get the moveable staircase in place. Baron decided to use his time to get the conversation out of the way. He met Ajax's narrowed gaze with a raised brow and a tense jawline.

"I haven't said a thing about what we do for the Army," he gave Ajax a pointed look. "I invited her for dinner at my house that day after we saw all of that chaos at the refuge.

She came over to talk to me because her bosses and coworkers weren't taking her seriously. She was upset and needed to talk and get some of the pressure off of her shoulders."

When the noise from the hydraulics on the moveable stairway stopped, he turned to see who was going down the steps first.

No one was moving. They were all looking at him.

"What?"

Boss shook his head. "Well, that's a change."

Train chuckled. "Seismic. I'm surprised it didn't shake the Pacific Shelf and start a tsunami."

Baron lifted a hand and a middle finger at Train. "Mind your own business."

Train shrugged. "This is more fun."

Feeling something odd twist inside of his chest, Baron glared at the man. "Don't you have a wedding to plan?"

Train's expression softened. He'd proposed to Ku'uipo during Christmas last year. They were likely having some kind of epic wedding. Between Train's love of movies and Ku'uipo's talent as a dancer, Baron wouldn't be surprised if they ended up recreating the wedding from Blue Hawaii since they'd fallen in love on the island of Kauai where they'd filmed the movie.

And with all of that to deal with, Train shouldn't even bother worrying about his non-relationship with Mahina.

"She's going to wonder where you've been."

Baron started down the stairs, tossing a quick look over his shoulder at Cullen. "She spends a lot of time with Olena."

Cullen jogged down the steps and came up beside Baron, the two of them walking together. "So what? Olena doesn't know where we go, but she knows why we're out of contact."

Baron shrugged as his booted foot hit the tarmac. "Whatever she knows probably comes from Olena. If Olena's kept it from her, it's not like she'd ask me about it."

"It's not like she's had the chance to ask." Cullen jogged up to his side and put a hand on his shoulder to hold him back. "Do have a plan of what you're going to do now that you're back?"

Baron shrugged his hand off of his shoulder and stepped back. "What's your problem, man? We just got off the damn plane! I haven't even had a minute on my own to think, let alone care, about what you think I need to do."

The others in the team walked on by, but Ajax hung back to watch, no doubt worried that one, or both of them, would take a swing at the other.

"You're an ass."

Baron shrugged. "No secret there."

"No, this isn't something to joke about."

Joke?

Baron felt the edges of his vision go dark.

He wasn't joking about anything, he just didn't think it was any of his business what he was doing with Mahina.

He wouldn't step over any damn line that she drew in the sand. She was a woman grown and he was a man. That fact was driven home every damn time he was close enough to see her.

Those deep brown eyes.

Her elegant face and gently curving body.

And her mind.

He didn't have to know what was going on inside of her brain to know that she was fucking brilliant. Baron swore he could feel it in the air around her when he got close enough to touch or smell the soft herbal scents that she wore.

Hell, it was probably a sunscreen or some kind of lotion, but regardless of what it was, her scent made him ache.

And yeah, he'd been just about to cross that line when he got the alert and had to leave her in his home.

He owed her some kind of apology. He knew it wasn't going to be a good one. He'd never learned that skill growing up and never thought he'd care to figure out how to get better at it, ever.

But he'd seen the look on her face and shit. For the first time in his life, he'd wanted to turn back around and explain why he had to go, even though he knew that he couldn't.

The look on her face, the loss of her warmth, he still felt it.

And as much as he could miss another person, he missed her.

"What's going on, Baron?"

He looked up at Cullen and bit down on the inside of his cheek.

"Oh good, the silent treatment."

"Don't be an ass, Cullen." Baron felt something pinch between his shoulder blades, a strange, painful sensation. "That's my job."

His friend chuckled. "You could teach a fucking master class."

"It's true." Baron nodded. "You think they'd pay me for something like that?"

Silence fell between them as the others walked off, and then Cullen gave him a look that said he could see right through Baron's shit.

"Seriously, Baron. What's going on?"

Baron fought back against the anger that started to boil up inside of him again. "It's not any of your business."

Cullen clapped a hand down on his shoulder and the grip he had hurt just enough that Baron had to make the conscious decision not to throw his friend's hand off of his shoulder. They were both trained to fight. They knew how to defend and they knew how to cause pain, injury, and even death.

There's no way he'd go that far over his teammate sticking his damn nose in where it didn't belong, but causing his friend a little pain? There wasn't a rule against it.

Well, unless Olena found out, because she'd kick Baron's ass.

He looked Cullen in the eye and shook his head. "We're both adults, Cullen."

"You better not fuck her over."

The devil on Baron's shoulder just couldn't pass up a setup like that one, but for the first time in forever, his other shoulder was occupied by a god damn angel who told him he didn't need to be his worst self to get his point across.

Cullen folded his arms across his chest. "What, you're not going to make some kind of an off-color joke? You're not going to be an ass and prove you're an asshole yet again?"

"Look, man. I'm not going to argue with you. I want to go get a damn shower. I want to go and find Mahina and figure out if she even wants to hear whatever bullshit excuse I'm going to have to make up so that she doesn't know exactly what we do for the Army. So, no. I'm not going to say the lewd and rude thing that was in my head."

He saw Cullen lift an eyebrow at his words.

"Yeah, I thought it. I'm an asshole, remember?"

"Then why not say it, Baron? I've seen you have your share, and then some, of indiscriminate ass."

"I'd like to say I'm a better man than I used to be," he gave Cullen a knowing nod, "but we both know I'd be full of shit."

Cullen nodded back. "You're always full of shit."

That got a smile from Baron. "No argument there."

"So, what are you going to do?"

Baron lifted both hands and started ticking off on his fingers. "Shower. Find Mahina. After that, fuck if I know."

Cullen gave him a look. "I mean it, man. Mahina's a damn good person. If you fuck with her, I'll kick your ass."

Shrugging his shoulders, Baron nodded. "Normally, I'd say 'You and whose Army,' but I know what Army you'd use and I bet your woman would go straight for my balls."

Cullen nailed him with a look. "I don't know what's likely to get you in more trouble. You talking about Olena and your balls in the same breath or you insinuating that it would take more than 'Lena and I to kick your ass."

Baron hadn't expected to smile at Cullen's words.

"You can try, Cullen. You sure can try."

NINE

When they reached the parking lot at the entrance to Kaena Point, Mahina's Lyft driver looked up in the rearview mirror and asked her, "Are you going hiking now?"

And then, before she managed an answer, he continued on.

"Alone? Are you sure?"

She really wasn't. Not deep down.

And given her argument with Olena a few days ago, she knew what she was doing was likely stupid, but no one was taking her seriously at work.

Or at least they weren't willing to take a stand with her against Milton's dismissive comments and the off-color jokes he'd been making around the office.

When Mahina realized that the driver was still looking at her, she tried to make him feel better.

At least it would be one of them, right?

"I'm meeting someone."

A quirked eyebrow told her that she wasn't fooling anyone.

"Right. Well, you can always ask for another ride away from here at any time."

"Uh... thanks. But, I'm okay."

She opened the back door and stepped out. When she closed the door, the driver rolled down the passenger window.

"Miss?"

She looked back at the man, bending to the side a little to see in through the window. The man still looked concerned. He held out a water bottle toward her. "Here. Please take this. You might need it."

She gestured at the backpack that she'd just shrugged into. "I have water in my pack."

He stretched out his arm and shook the bottle. "Please, Miss. Take this."

Groaning inside, she reached out and took the bottle of water. "Thank you."

"You're welcome, I guess." He shrugged. "Just please, call for another ride when you change your mind."

She lifted her free hand to wave at him and she walked away before he could try to convince her again.

Mahina passed by the Welcome sign which listed the rules for use of the public area outside of the refuge, including the 'NO VEHICLES PAST THIS POINT' rule. And right beside it, through a space someone had opened up, rolling away the boulders that had been placed there, wheel treads wide enough to be a large truck dug into the dirt.

She shook her head.

"Off roaders."

Mahina had seen the reports. Read through all the statements. Locals, tourists, even the military off duty had driven their cars onto the dirt to 'off-road' around the boulders and into the sandy area beyond the parking lot.

She wanted to roll the boulder back into place, but even she knew that she didn't have the strength for the job.

A fleeting thought brought a discomfiting wave of emotion through her.

Her immediate thought had been to ask Baron if he could get his friends, the other men in his unit, to help.

But she had no idea where he was.

Or when he'd come back.

She swallowed hard as another voice popped up in her head. It joined the litany of other unwelcome and uncharitable voices that plagued her from time to time.

Maybe he's back and he just doesn't want to see you?

Well, that would suck, she agreed, but it wasn't like they had a relationship.

She blinked back tears as she squeezed past the locked gate and walked along the utility road.

It was true. She knew that.

He'd invited her for dinner because she was upset. He was just being nice.

Mahina heard Olena's voice in her head. "Baron's not a nice guy."

"He's not like Cullen." Mahina argued back in her head. "But she hadn't really seen any evidence that Baron was as bad as the others made him out to be. Even when she'd been around the whole unit for a day at the beach, she'd heard the men making jokes about his reputation as the ass.

The women laughed it off easily with knowing looks, but Mahina had never seen anything herself to warrant the comments, but Baron hadn't tried to argue it either.

He'd just lifted his chin and smiled at the others or shrugged off other comments.

And he'd barely noticed her at all, which is what gave her the opportunity to look at him over the top of her book.

He was built like the other guys. Strong. Muscled. The

total package physically. And yes, she'd taken a look... there. After all, there was that magic 'V' that people talked about. And that V was definitely pointing... there.

When he was wearing board shorts and playing beach volleyball with some of the others it wasn't hard to notice that even with that mesh thing that guys had in their shorts, he was big enough that it only made things... more noticeable.

Nervous and in need of something to do with her hands, Mahina opened the bottle of water that the ride-share driver had given her and lifted it to her lips. She barely dribbled a few drops over her bottom lip and into her mouth.

She tried to ignore the way her hands were shaking, but then again, that was the easiest thing to focus on as she kept moving.

It didn't take long for her to reach the spot that she'd scoped out before while working at the site. On the mauka, the mountain side, of the road, there was a natural trench that was deep enough for her to lie down or slouch into and she wouldn't be seen above the road.

She took off her backpack and dropped it down into the trench and left it there as she moved over to the fence that protected the refuge site.

The fence had been mended since the last 'event' as Milton called it. Mended but not fixed entirely. It was an expensive thing to do, she knew. She'd seen the cost sheets the last time they'd replaced that section of the fence.

It wasn't an amount of money that she could afford on her own. Something built to protect the area from all manner of rodents and other wild animals had to be strong and nearly impossible to nibble or claw through.

Materials like that weren't cheap.

Digging into her pocket, she withdrew the key and opened the lock on the gate. She knew she had to check on the albatrosses as part of her duties, but she really enjoyed her time amongst them as a person. Someone who loves nature and admires it.

Once through the gate, she locked it up behind her and put the key back into her pocket, withdrawing a folded garbage bag as well.

Mahina made her way around the area, picking up bits of trash that had probably blown in over the top of the fence. She couldn't stand the thought of one of the birds eating it by accident.

A few bits of paper were all that she found, carefully picking them up, using the bag over her hands to keep her hands clean. She had a package of wipes in her pack, and a trash bag to put them in and 'pack them out' if she used them.

The last thing she wanted to do was chance leaving behind trash.

A little squeak of sound turned her head and she saw the snowy white head of an albatross looking up at her from its nest. Her egg wasn't visible from the angle she could see from, but it didn't matter.

The albatross was safe, and if she was incubating her egg to hatch it, she wouldn't move.

Mahina gave the mother a nod and smiled.

Without checking the coded leg band, she couldn't make sure that it was the albatross she was thinking of, but most of the birds nesting in the area had been laying and hatching eggs for a handful of years. Enough time to be well versed in what it took to bring their babies into the world.

It was just up to Mahina and the others working under DLNR to help keep them safe enough to give them that time.

"Hey, there."

The albatross made soft grunting noises and another bird lifted her head a few feet away.

"Sorry, ladies. I didn't mean to disturb you." She moved away and picked up a few more pieces of trash.

One disturbing piece was the remnants of a cigarette.

Mahina picked it up with the trash bag over her hand and looked at the offending piece of trash.

Whoever had smoked it had taken their time. And then they'd discarded it.

She really hoped that it had somehow been carried by the wind. Or maybe, and this wasn't what she hoped had happened, another bird had picked it up in its beak and brought it over the fence.

Shaking her head, she moved on, hoping that it wasn't something that she'd find regularly, but that was the problem. People breaking into the refuge area would always bring trouble. Sometimes it would be trash. Sometimes the outright destruction of the land and with it, the birds.

Sometimes it was just people being careless.

And sometimes it was just plain, idiotic entitlement. People did what they wanted because they wanted it. They didn't care about how that affected others. And people like that cared even less about the natural world around them.

Mahina wanted people to care.

They might never care like she did, but that was true of so many things, but it didn't mean that people could destroy something thinking it didn't matter. They might not see why it was important, but it was. With the aid of the fence keeping out predators, the population of albatrosses had grown at the refuge.

They laid their eggs and fed their young, and that meant they'd come back and build more nests. It would be rewarding to see what things would look like in a couple of years and then again in a couple more.

People owed it to the albatrosses to give them a chance to thrive in the world and Mahina was looking forward to seeing that happened at Kaena point with her help. Her mom had always said that she should try to do better. Be better.

And working at the refuge made her feel like she was finally doing that.

"All right, ladies. I'm going to pack out this trash and hope that this is the most interesting thing that happens here tonight."

As she walked away, she felt a cold sensation crawling up her spine.

She'd done the math, or rather, she'd plotted things out on a calendar and it all ended up in one interesting direction.

Darkness.

New Moons if you followed the phases of the moon.

She was there, planning to stay the night, and if she was right, get some proof that this wasn't careless tourists or apathetic locals. This wasn't just people out to have fun, drinking themselves stupid.

As she climbed down into the trench, she saw that her cell phone screen was glowing. A call was coming in from Olena.

A call that was going to go unanswered.

She didn't need another person trying to tell her no.

If she was right, and she prayed that she was wrong, people were doing this, hiding this... whatever they were doing, it wasn't good for anyone and Mahina was going to find a way to stop it.

IT WAS dark when Baron got home and got in the shower. He knew something that would help him feel better. Scrubbing his skin red and raw helped. The abrading pain woke him up better than coffee and even though the team was supposed to relax, he knew he had to see Mahina and figure out just how pissed off she was at him.

It had been a relief to get back to his house at Schofield Base. That relief had never been something he sought before. He'd always looked forward to traveling and discovering places he'd never been. When he first joined the Army, it was the adventure that he looked forward to. Testing himself physically was a bonus.

Feeling like an outsider hadn't bothered him at all. In fact, it was that feeling that made him feel like things were right. In his own home, as long as he could remember, he'd felt like the odd one out.

And the frustration under the surface dimmed a little when he was traveling.

Well, it had, before.

Traveling halfway around the world didn't hold the allure it used to.

He still like the challenges that the job presented. Baron liked doing things that were difficult. Hard.

That was who he was, anyway. He was difficult.

His nature wasn't easy or accepting.

And it was only the fact that his team put up with him that kept him around.

He picked up the towel that hung over the showerhead and rubbed it against the bar of soap, building up a good lather before he put that rough towel against his skin. He'd clean himself off and then he'd go and find Mahina and hope that she could forgive him for being away so long.

And not need any real explanation for where they'd gone.

Because the others were right. Their women knew who they were and what they did, but Mahina wasn't that yet.

Yet.

He shook his head and heard the droplets of water land on the tile walls.

He wasn't looking for what the others had. He couldn't give that kind of power to anyone over his life.

People that close to you hurt you that much more. His father had been a practical example of that. One that was in his face and impossible to miss.

He wasn't the kind of man who could be more than a friend or a passionate distraction for a woman. Especially someone like Mahina.

She was too damn pure for an ass like him, but that didn't stop him from wanting a taste of that sweetness. And it sure as hell didn't stop him from wanting to get his hands all over her body and his...

He turned the water up, harder and hotter.

Baron had to stop thinking about it before he ended up staying in the shower longer with this fist around his dick.

He wanted... No. He *needed* to see her.

Consequences be damned.

He had to see Mahina and find out if she was still talking to him.

BARON TOOK a chance and called Mahina's phone, but of course, it went to voicemail. He hadn't been in contact with her for a while so no, of course he didn't expect anything, he just didn't know where to go from nowhere.

He dialed Olena next. She'd know something.

And maybe she'd throw him a bone and let him know what, if anything, Mahina had told her about his absence.

The call picked up almost instantly.

"Baron! Where are you?"

His instinct was to say something flippant or asinine. Olena was used to flinging them back at him. He held back though, hearing something in her voice that he wasn't used to.

Panic.

"I'm driving toward you guys. I wanted to talk to Mahina. Is she there with her mom?"

A moment of silence was punctuated with a muttered curse.

"No. Her mother is here with my mom. I called because I think Mahina might be in trouble."

Baron pulled off on the side of the road and picked his phone up off of the dashboard mount and brought it closer. "What's going on?"

"I thought if I told her to wait... if I told her that I wouldn't go with her, she wouldn't do it... and-"

"What's going on? What did she want to do?"

"I think she's going to try and prove that people are sneaking into the wildlife refuge to cause trouble."

"Why didn't you... " Why, what? He didn't bother asking her why she didn't stop her friend. Mahina was a grown woman with a mind of her own and likely, if she wanted to go she would do it. "When did you find out she was gone?"

He heard Olena gasp in a breath.

"I've been cooking since I heard from Cullen that you guys came back today so I haven't been up to the other house. She must have dropped her mom off earlier. Baron, I didn't know."

"Hey, hey... The important thing is getting to her so she's safe. So you think she's at Kaena Point?"

"She checked the dates and it's after the new moon nights when they've found the damage."

Baron looked out of his window at the sky. Besides a few pinpoints of light in the sky, that was it. The moon wasn't visible.

"Okay, so she's up there tonight. I'm still in Wahiawa. I'll head up there."

"We can start up there in a few minutes."

Baron heard Cullen on the other end of the line cautioning Olena. For the sake of expedience, Baron added his own concerns as he put his car in drive and headed for another gate at Schofield. It was faster than trying to U turn at night in the crowded streets. "You stay put. It'll probably be easier to keep this to a minimum number of people. Without the moon, it'll be easier to move around in the dark if it's just me. But if you've got a substation out there near the park, you might want to give them a call and have them be at the ready in case we do find the people responsible."

Olena started to argue, but she stopped a moment later. "You'll take care of her?"

He sat back as he approached the gate, waiting for the guards to wave him through.

"Baron?" He heard the tension in her voice and felt the answering sensation in his chest. "Will you bring her home safe?"

"I'll do whatever it takes or die trying."

He meant every damn word.

TEN

If there was one thing she didn't take into consideration, it was the inability to tell what time it was. If the moon was up, she could have traced it through the sky.

With a new moon, she was stuck, quite literally, in the dark.

The minutes... hours? crawled on by and as she lay there in the trench, she had second, third, and fourth thoughts about what she'd done.

With her hands, she moved over the items that she'd brought out of her pack. A small, almost miniscule tripod to steady her cell phone.

She'd downloaded and tested the NiteEyes app on her iPhone.

And to know where to shoot? She'd brought... borrowed Olena's night-vision goggles.

She'd asked about them when she remembered a conversation they'd had about a stakeout where Olena had been unable to follow their suspects because the light had been too low in the back-alleys of Chinatown. After that, she'd bought a pair of night vision goggles to use in future investigations.

And it was that very pair that Mahina had taken without permission from her friend.

She hoped that Olena wouldn't hate her too much. She just needed to make sure that she had an edge.

If these people were breaking into the refuge to destroy it, then she had to see them and get some kind of photographic proof.

The photos may even make it possible to identify them.

That, she sighed, would be a dream.

While her test of the low-light app on her phone had been half-way decent, it didn't guarantee a clear image of faces, but at least it would be good enough to prove her theory.

And if no one showed up? Well, she'd likely have a few mosquito bites and pain in her back and her neck.

Still, no one else from her office knew that she was planning to be there overnight. They couldn't mock what they didn't know.

She certainly wasn't clocking in since this was her own decision.

Mahina hoped beyond hope that it was going to be worth it.

HE WAS GOING to kill Mahina.

Okay, not kill her. That would be to conspicuous.

Olena would know and that would start a whole vendetta thing. Not worth it.

He felt the right side of his upper lip curl in a sneer. He was joking, sort of.

But he was mad as fuck.

He'd been gone for too long.

If he'd been there... if they'd had a chance to get to know each other better, he knew that she would have come to him and he would have gone with her.

He'd be there right now instead of driving with his hands white-knuckled on the steering wheel.

Moderately high speed. Keeping an eye out for other cars and people. Even then his mind was in a whirl.

He'd been there on the property enough. He'd seen her working at the refuge again and again, so he knew the stretch of the road she'd be hiding near.

There was a bit of a trench on the mountain side of the road.

Mauka.

He heard the word in his head. He'd lived in Hawaii long enough to know some of the vernacular. And that included directions.

Living in Hawaii for at least a few years, you picked up a number of the local lingo and phrases.

In Hawaii, the kanaka or kama'aina didn't talk about north, east, south, and west much when giving directions. One of the ladies had explained it to him a while back. Given that the islands were volcanic in nature, there were basically two directions that people used.

Mauka which was mountainside.

Makai which was waterside.

So he would find his way through the dark along the road and look for her on the mountainside of the well-worn stretch of dirt road.

Thank god he'd been just outside of the base walls. He'd turned around and grabbed up a bag of equipment and changed his pants and shoes to black, matching his Henley shirt. He had everything he needed to blend into the darkness, but he wasn't sure he'd be able to keep quiet once he found her.

He was only too eager to find her and make sure she got out of there safely.

Then what?

He turned onto the road that led along the coast and found himself struggling to answer that question to his own satisfaction.

Talking to her wasn't going to be enough.

They'd still talk, but he was going to make damn sure she was too exhausted to argue with him.

Yeah, he was planning to lay down the law.

He just didn't know what the rules were going to be besides keeping her within arm's length for the rest of his life.

Knowing she was out there, alone, possibly in danger, was killing him inside.

Warning bells went off in his head. This was a far cry from what he always told himself. He was fine getting balls deep in a woman, but he didn't let her get under his skin.

And Mahina...

Well, she wasn't just *getting* under his skin, she was already there.

He was good and truly fucked.

WHEN SHE STARTED to nod off, she'd started pinching herself to keep awake. Mahina had no idea what she thought she'd do to keep awake.

Details like that hadn't really factored into her thinking.

She knew she wasn't like Olena in that aspect.

Her friend was so detail oriented that she probably had plan after plan detailing all of her options to keep her mind active and awake.

It didn't help that the night before she'd barely had any sleep. Her mother had been up and down all night long.

She'd complained about the music playing when there was no music. And then, around two in the morning, she'd started cooking something on the stove and then gone back to sleep.

If Mahina hadn't been tossing and turning enough to smell the acrid scent of smoldering food on the stove, her mother might have burned down their house.

By the time she'd fallen asleep, exhausted by the stress, it was time to get up again.

Thank goodness she had an appointment with a non-profit in a couple of days. They were funding different care options for families in dire need. Mahina wasn't sure that they qualified in part or at all, but she was more than willing to fill out piles of paperwork if it meant that her mother could get the kind of care she needed.

Mahina felt like she was walking a tightrope at the moment. Taking care of her mother required resources that she didn't have.

Her mother's doctor had really come through, finding a federal non-profit with money to spare for patients with dementia.

As her thoughts shifted more toward her mother, the building anxiety inside of her was going to make it easier to stay awake. After all, that was part of the reason why she'd hardly slept the night before and the nights before that.

Being a failure in the eyes of your mother was hard to deal with. Aunt Lynn and Olena kept telling her that she was doing a great job, but they were just trying to make her feel better.

If she was doing a good job, then she wouldn't need her aunt's help for several days a week. Aunt Lynn still had a child at home. Sure, he was a teen, but he was still in school and there was only so much help she could get from her aunt before it put a strain on their relationship.

A wind blew off of the ocean and up toward the mountains. There was enough that it swirled into the trench and she was surrounded by a bone deep chill.

She wrapped her arms around herself and rubbed at her back and upper arm, trying to spread the warmth through her extremities.

Another wind, coupled with the crashing sound of waves against the rocks, and she was suddenly questioning her luck.

It was already bad, but being buffeted by wind carrying pebbles and leaves wasn't making it any better.

No sign of the men, or women, who had been vandalizing the refuge. She just had to hunker down and wait.

And shiver.

She knew she had to come and try to stop the damage that was being done. She just wished she wasn't doing it alone.

Drawing her knees up toward her chest, Mahina wrapped her arms around her legs and held them close. At least this way she made the smallest target for the wind.

Mahina put her forehead down on her knees and fought back the tears.

She had to hold it together just until daylight. Then, she could leave and regroup, ask Olena again or maybe... just maybe... talk to Baron when his unit came back to Hawaii.

Squeezing her eyes shut, she let herself whisper the question she needed the answer to more than anything else.

"Baron, where are you?"

She went stock still as she felt warmth surround her, hands on top of her own.

Part of her wanted to scream out for help, but she didn't.

She felt heat surrounding her body, warming her back and her arms.

When she felt the tender kiss pressed against her cheek, she thought she was fast asleep and dreaming.

"I'm right here, baby. Now, let me get you warm."

ELEVEN

There had been room enough for her on her own with her pack, but before he got down in the trench with her, he knew it was going to be a tight fit.

Wearing black from head to toe, he was covered, keeping the wind off of his skin and anything visible on his face he'd covered with black camo-stick paint.

Moving as quietly as he'd been trained to do, she hadn't heard or sensed him until he was beside her.

And that, he reasoned, was for the best.

If he'd made noise and startled her in a different way, she might have called out or scrambled away from him. Either of those options might have revealed herself to anyone skulking around in the dark.

Adjusting her body so she was stretched out beside him, he pulled of his night-vision goggles and set them aside where he could reach them when it was needed.

She shifted against him and the subtle friction didn't make things easier for him.

They made them harder.

She made them harder.

"W-when did you come back?"

"A few hours ago."

"A few... okay."

A wind coursed over them and he felt some strands of her hair whip across his chin.

He hated that he was wearing gloves to hide his hands, but he couldn't resist the urge to touch her. He brushed his fingertips across her skin and smoothed her hair behind her ear. "I heard from Olena that you might be here, so here I am."

"So, you came because of Olena."

He heard her tone flatten a little and her body tense a little against him.

Baron touched his hand to the side of her face and, turning his hand, he traced a knuckle down her cheek to the delicate line of her jaw.

It was pitch dark without the moon. Despite that, he swore he could *see* her in his mind.

"I came here for you, Mahina."

Leaning over her, he placed a soft kiss against her lips.

"I missed you the whole time we were gone." He let out his breath so he could breathe in her scent, turning his head to the side so that their cheeks were nearly touching. "I hated that I couldn't tell you where we were or what we were doing."

"Olena said you were deployed."

He felt a muscle tick in his cheek. It was the truth in a way. It just wasn't exactly what was going on.

"But you weren't, were you?" He heard the pain in her tone, but he didn't know what it was for exactly. "I might not know what Olena and the other women know about you and the other men, where you are at times, but I know that deployments aren't just for a couple of weeks. They didn't even give you a chance to say goodbye to the people who would worry about you."

Baron dropped his chin to his chest and ground his teeth together. He'd done that to her.

He'd left like her like that.

It wouldn't have been such a shock for the other women. Even Tehani who was the newest woman to be folded into the group, knew what it meant when they got 'the call.'

"I'm sorry, I didn't expect it to happen."

He let out breath through his nose and winced at the odd sensation his own words made in his chest.

Sorry wasn't something he said easily. Or hardly ever.

It grated on his nerves when others expected it of him.

He said what he meant and there weren't many people or situations that would cause him to use the word.

But he knew Mahina was on that list.

Thinking that he made her worry or suffer got to him. He felt that worry like a stab to his gut and after that first biting pain, he felt the twist of it to the point where it almost stole his breath.

Why should it be any different from the other times he'd felt that pain, watching her from a distance?

He wanted her.

Wanted to protect her.

Wanted to take the pain that he saw darkening her features and wipe it from the earth.

She could and would do so much better in life than him, but for the moment, for the near future, he wanted to touch her and make her smile.

He knew he couldn't keep up the ruse of being a good guy for long, his need for her wouldn't allow him to stay away, but deep inside he knew that she deserved better than him.

And he'd let her go so she could find that, but he wanted her first.

He wanted to take care of her and pretend as long as he could keep up the ruse, not because he wanted to fool her.

He wanted to believe that he could be that kind of guy no matter what example his father had set. And maybe he could... for a little while.

Unlike his dad, he could make the effort to be better, he just knew it wasn't going to stick.

Mahina reached for his hand and caught it probably from blind luck. "I was worried. When I didn't hear from you. I was worried."

Well, shit.

He would have welcomed anger.

A slap would have been fine.

A punch he could have handled.

But worry?

The way she was holding his hand. Tight. Squeezing. Drawing it up between them. It all knocked him off balance.

"And when Olena wouldn't tell me anything besides how normal everything was, I it was even worse. I didn't even know if something happened to you if they'd say anything to me."

Baron had the feeling that she wouldn't be saying any of this if they were sitting somewhere with the lights on. Mahina wasn't someone who let her feelings out very often. He'd seen her swallow her emotions in public situations before.

"There are some things you can't know. Not with the way things are." He swore he could feel her tense up, pull away. "I wish I could explain more, but-"

Baron heard the soft thump of something against rock.

Something unnatural.

Something man made.

Mahina heard it too.

She was still beside him and when he reached out and

picked up his night-vision goggles, he felt her move. She'd left her goggles on the edge of the trench and he could see them. Baron picked them up and helped her to put them on.

Leaning down, he whispered into her ear. "Is that your camera?"

She turned and almost knocked her goggles off of her face.

Baron steadied her and moved a little to the side to give her as much room as he could in the roadside trench.

He saw the hint of a smile on her lips and watched as she quickly set up her phone on its tripod.

Leaning to the side, he saw that she'd hidden most of the phone behind some rocks. It left just a sliver of the phone along with the lens of the camera uncovered.

As long as someone wasn't looking for surveillance, they wouldn't see it.

They just needed to see who was coming through the refuge and causing the damage that was upsetting Mahina so much.

Once everything was set up and the camera was recording, Mahina slouched down into the trench.

He moved down so that his body was braced over hers.

If someone came to the road and looked over, they might be seen, and if that happened, he had his sidearm.

If it came down to it, he'd defend her with deadly force and not have a single second thought about it.

There were few absolute certainties in his life.

Having her six was one of those. He could and would do whatever it took to protect her. Not knowing what was coming out of the ocean made him nervous. He wasn't afraid for himself.

He was afraid for the people causing the damage if they posed any immediate threat to the woman pressed against him.

Baron knew he could do some real damage to anyone that meant her harm.

Smiling in the dark, he included himself in that statement.

"Now we wait."

WAIT.

Mahina would have no problem waiting, normally.

But laying under Baron, unable to move, was torture.

Abject torture.

She'd dreamed of being under him entirely too much to pretend that she didn't want to be right where she was, but with dirt and rocks at her back and Olena's heavy night-vision goggles covering most of her face, she felt like she was a background character in a Star Trek BORG episode who only needed her face covered to fit into the scene.

So, trying to keep motionless, when all she wanted to do was move, felt like hell.

Baron leaned over her, his cheek almost against hers. "Stay still and breathe slowly. They're coming."

With her face to the sky, she knew she couldn't see anything, so she closed her eyes and listened.

Something scraped against the rocks again in the ocean. There were reefs all around the beach that would make it difficult for a boat to get anywhere close to it so she could only imagine what was happening.

It was one thing to make educated guesses about what was happening when it was daytime and the sun was up.

Now, in the dark of night, it felt like a nightmare. Every sound was magnified and the silences felt like black holes.

"You're tensing up, babe. Breathe."

She wanted to nod, but she knew that he was close and

she didn't want to hit him in the head or knock off her goggles.

Instead, she took a breath and tried to relax, but she couldn't seem to do it.

That's when she felt Baron's hand on her hip and his thumb stroking her belly.

She melted under him with just that touch and together they waited.

And waited.

Until they heard voices and heavy footsteps.

Mahina bit into her bottom lip, trying to keep silent as they walked along the road, headed for the entrance to the park. She wanted to do something to stop them, but they could hear three voices speaking back and forth to each other.

She could feel herself smiling even though the damage they might be leaving behind was nothing to smile about, but now she had video proof.

She wasn't imagining things.

Relief flooded through her and she pulled the night-vision goggles off of her head, laying back in the dirt.

Beside her, Baron reached down for something and a moment later she could see his phone.

The bulk of his body would easily hide the low-light from his dimmed screen.

"'Lena?"

Mahina sat up, bracing herself on her elbows.

"Yeah. She was right. Three men from what we can hear. Send in the cavalry." He paused, listening. "Yeah. I'll tell her, but let your guys know that I'll be bringing up the rear. Dark clothes. Night-vision goggles. Asshole attitude on full display."

He lowered the phone but left it on so she was able to see some of his features.

"Promise me you'll stay here until I come back for you."

Mahina lifted her chin and looked up into his face. "I'm going to stay right here."

He smiled and her heart clenched in her chest. "And later, I'm going to answer all of your questions."

She heard his words and nodded, not wanting to argue with him in anyway.

Whoever those men were, they could be very, very dangerous. The last thing she wanted to do was pull Baron's focus away from the confrontation.

Before he could move away, she reached out and made contact with his hand.

"Baron?" She was barely whispering, determined not to alert anyone that they were there in the trench. "Please, be careful."

It was a moment before he moved, but in that moment, she thought she heard him cursing under his breath.

"Stay here, baby. I'll be back before you know it."

And then he was gone.

SITTING IN HIS OFFICE, Sato looked at the medical records for Suzume.

He shook his head and stared out into the dark night sky over the ocean. The man who brought him the file had left as soon as he was able. He didn't even wait to be excused.

Paging through the medical file was as enlightening as it was maddening.

For years, his father told him that Suzume and his daughter were well taken care of. He'd been shown report after report detailing their lives in Hawaii. It was the only reason why he didn't try to take control from his father.

He was told that they were happy. Healthy.

Waiting for him to fulfill his father's wishes first.

He picked up the photo taken by the hospital on the day that Mahina was born. She had the typical ink black hair that would be expected from his child, and her eyes were dark, watchful.

He remembered his father's voice from their conversation from the day that they received word that Mahina was born.

"Now you have a child."

His father's tone was cold. Distant.

"A girl."

Sato didn't have the outlook that his father did. Having a girl wasn't a death sentence. There could always be more children. Another chance to have a boy.

"It would be one thing if you had produced a boy. Your lack of discipline would have had some benefit to the family."

He'd held his tongue, barely.

His father who had such a distasteful reaction to the birth of a granddaughter had doted on his own daughter, Sato's younger sister.

The same sister who had taken her own life when she discovered her father's criminal enterprise and the blood that stained his hands.

"I want to see them, father."

"What you want," he'd lowered his voice, almost hissing at him, "is irrelevant. You have a duty to represent our family. A duty to follow my orders. Isn't it enough that your philandering has ruined your first chance at an advantageous marriage, Jun? The lengths that I went to, finding a woman of a well to do family, a woman who understood her place, a woman who would bear you sons and raise them in the right way. You failed me, Jun. And it will be your last failure if you want to take over from me someday."

Suzume wasn't part of a failure.

She was beautiful. She was educated. And she made him happy.

He smiled when he was with her.

"I'll never understand," his father shook his head and glared at him, "how you could dirty your hands with a woman from America. You... We," he insisted, "are better than that."

"I will marry who you want, father."

His father's cutting glare told him how ridiculous he was for saying the words. His father's orders were just that. He was expected to follow. And after his father discovered that he'd created a child with a woman that he didn't approve of, Sato's father had made it understood that any other mistakes on Sato's part would be the end of their relationship in so many ways.

The end of so many things.

And so he left Suzume alone to raise their daughter, trusting the reports he'd received.

Trusting that his father would uphold his end of their very lop-sided bargain.

How was he to know that so very much of those reports were fabricated?

Over the last few years, as his father had begun to deteriorate both mentally and physically, Sato had taken more and more of the business into his control, moving men like chess pieces around the board.

Including, moving himself to the head of all the enterprises in Hawaii. Even then, he had waited for his father to die before deciding to enter Suzume's life again. To do so when his father might still hear about his new indiscretions would have been dangerous with his father's more quixotic emotions as he struggled with his own illness.

Now, he finally had a chance to acknowledge his family

only to find out that Suzume was suffering from the same kind of illness that had taken his father's life.

A wry smile twisted at the corners of his mouth. How ironic was it that the woman his father wanted to keep out of his life shared the same struggle?

His gaze moved to the clock on the wall and he sat back in his chair. One of his crews was using the darkness of the new moon to smuggle in a monster sized shipment of fentanyl. The men were bringing them in on boats to the water just outside of Kaena Point park and the wildlife refuge.

Wrapped in waterproof skins, they floated them in and carried them over the rocks. The fence had been repaired, but the men were carrying wire cutters strong enough to break through the fence.

From there, they would hike out to the road to be picked up by trucks waiting nearby for that very purpose.

From one night alone, the smuggled contraband would be worth hundreds of thousands of dollars, enough to give his daughter a gift that would make sure she saw the value of his work.

A gift that should ensure her compliance.

He drew a photo out from under the medical file and set it on top of the pile. Mahina on the day of her graduation from Stanford University.

She cared about her work. That was evidenced in the comments he'd heard from their man inside DLNR. Milton Ching was frustrated at her dogged determination to stop the intermittent damage done to the nesting site.

While Milton had been told to find a way to stop her interference, secretly, Sato admired his daughter's determination.

If it wasn't his operations that she was trying to interfere with, he would champion her actions and her dogged defense of the wildlife area.

Milton had assured his representative that Mahina wouldn't create problems for them much longer. It might be a difficult blow for her to take in her young career, but the money that he earned from these smuggling activities?

He'd give her a portion of the profit, or perhaps he'd fund a job for her somewhere else. Another animal, another refuge for her to defend.

He'd make it worth her while to walk away in the end.

He had the patience to do that for her.

He'd waited her whole life to meet her and spend time with her, he might even convince her that she didn't need a job. She could travel with him. Spend time with him and enjoy the best that the world had to offer.

He could make up for the time they'd been apart because of his own father.

But first, he looked back at the clock. He was waiting for news on the shipment of fentanyl. Later, he'd plan what to do about Suzume and his daughter.

TWELVE

Baron removed his sidearm from his holster as he moved. He had a concealed carry permit for a handgun, but he was to tail a few guys out of a restricted wildlife refuge.

The wind that blew in across the nesting area cooled his cheek and made his skin itch under the camouflage colors that he'd applied to his skin. He wasn't sure what kind of approach the police would make, or if they'd get there at all before the men made an attempt to leave the park.

He would have to play it by ear, he realized.

He could easily take the three, especially if he crept up behind them. The element of surprise would help, but given their sizes and the look of their physiques, they'd put up a decent fight.

That might make the fight worth it.

Knowing the trouble that they'd caused Mahina, he was more than eager to take them apart, piece by piece.

For the moment, he was following them, waiting to see what would happen. If the police didn't show up in time to stop them, he was happy to follow the trio and see if he could identify a car or some other vehicle so he could turn the information in to the police.

Baron knew if it was just about himself and these men, he'd track them as long as he was physically able.

But it wasn't just himself.

He'd left Mahina behind to keep her safe, but he wasn't going to leave her alone for long.

The men ahead of him had their focus on the road ahead of them. He had to wonder how many times they'd done this very thing. They looked comfortable enough with the path. They hadn't even taken much time or energy to look around and see if they had company.

They were either really confident or really sloppy and Baron wasn't going to try and guess. Either option could be a problem.

Over confident came with its own pitfalls. He'd learned that the hard way.

The first time he'd ended up face first in the dirt during a hand to hand training was against one of the members of his own team. It had been his own fault. It happened a few more times before he'd learned his lesson, including a rather unfortunate photo of Shado, straddling his back with one arm bent at an awkward angle.

Someone still had a picture of it, of that he was sure.

It was a painful lesson, both physically and to his ego.

His father had driven home the thought that physically dominating someone showed just how badass you really were. A theory that Baron had unlearned over time.

A lot of that work had been during his time with his Delta team.

Being in the military was a family tradition, learning that his father had raised him to be a Class A asshole had been eye-opening, but it had also driven home the fact that he had a lot of emotional baggage that made him that much more tainted.

Cold.

Fucking ignorant when it came to love.

He certainly didn't know what that meant when it came to his need for Mahina.

It certainly had the potential to make him sloppy, ruminating over her.

And sloppy, well... sloppy meant danger.

Up ahead, he saw something change.

The man at the front of the trio nearly stopped, turning his head to look at the man behind him.

That left Baron in the middle of the road and the focus of the lead man of the group.

The man dropped the duffle bags that he was carrying and reached for his waistband.

Right.

Baron lifted his sidearm, aiming it at the man's head.

"Hands were I can see them."

Okay, so he wasn't a police officer, but he'd seen enough TV to make a half-baked attempt at it.

"All three of you." He kept the gun leveled at the man's head, but turned his head to make it clear that he was talking to all of them. "Bags down. Hands on your head."

He watched as the men complied.

He could see their furtive head movements as they looked at each other. The night-vision goggles they wore were similar to his own, heavier though. When they moved their heads, no matter how surreptitious they were trying to be, they had to work harder to turn their heads, and that made it more obvious.

Baron knew his best option at the moment was to keep the men off-balance, second guessing their situation.

Hopefully well enough that they won't wonder why he didn't identify himself as a police officer.

"Interlock your fingers."

Yes, watching COPS on YouTube came in handy.

The man to his right took a step back and Baron nailed him with a look from the corner of his eye.

"Don't," he told the man, "it's not worth the bullet."

The man grumbled under his breath. "Too cheap to use more than one?"

Baron took a moment to assess the scene and saw the duffle bag at the man's feet.

With a soft exhale, Baron pointed the gun down toward the ground and fired a shot.

The woven handle of the duffle bag split and the bullet buried itself in the dirt halfway to the feet of the man in the lead.

"What the fuck?" He flinched back but didn't jump or move his feet. "What the hell was that?"

"That," Baron felt a smile draw up the corners of his mouth, "was a warning shot. Just so you know, I won't need more than one for any of you. Don't test me."

The third man, who'd been silent until that moment, finally spoke up. "One against three? I'd call that decent odds."

"Speak for yourself, asshole."

Baron's smile broadened at their bickering. His team did the same thing, but they weren't the ones who got caught unawares. They were too fucking good for that.

"He's got the gun pointed at *my* head."

The third wheel spoke up again. "Like I said, decent odds. Besides, it's just him and us. We've got a chance to-"

Red and blue lights flared on and Baron saw the men react when two marked police vehicles pulled up behind a third vehicle with lights on the dash.

As the lead car's front doors flew open, Baron wanted to curse out loud. He pulled the night-vision goggles down past his chin so it hung around his neck.

Olena and her father stepped out of the car on either side.

Muttering under his breath, Baron hoped that this wasn't going to get either of them in trouble.

The uniformed officers moved forward to flank Olena and her dad. Their headlights illuminated the area and, given the way the men trapped between them turned their heads to the side, flinching away from the bright LED lamps, they were blinded by the lights.

That made it easier for the officers to get the men down on their knees and from there down on their stomachs.

Olena and her father didn't come anywhere near him until the men were carted off to the marked patrol cars and put in the cages, their hands cuffed behind them. That's when her father followed the officers and climbed into one of their cars and left the scene.

Once that happened, Cullen got out of the back seat of Olena's vehicle and made his way over.

Olena gave Cullen a soft smile before she turned back to Baron with a curiously raised eyebrow. "I'm not going to ask if that sidearm is registered, because I know it is."

Cullen folded his arms across his chest. "Was that shot we heard from you?"

Baron shrugged a shoulder. "I can't believe you had to ask. I wouldn't have let any of them get off a shot."

"Right now," she gestured at the road and the retreating taillights of the police cars, "my dad's headed to the local station to walk the men through booking. That, and he'll be trying to smooth things over with the brass at the station."

"You mean the guys who should have been on top of this instead of letting a scientist double as a LEO?"

"That," Olena pointed at him, "is exactly why it's my dad doing the talking."

Baron held up his hands in surrender. "No one ever said I should be the spokesperson of a damn thing besides the drink order at a bar." He held up a hand. "Let me go get Mahina."

Olena grinned at him before he turned away. "I was wondering where you'd hidden her.

"She already had a damn good hiding place before I even got here." He shook his head as he walked away.

He wasn't all that surprised that she'd been prepared, and even without a plan to involve the police, she had things under control. Even when he was driving toward the point, he knew that if she had gone to try her hand at a stakeout, Mahina wasn't going to just wing it.

She was too damn smart and she was going to be the end of him, tearing through his walls and certainly keeping him on his toes.

He had no idea what he was going to do with all of the extra energy he had arcing through his body. The adrenaline that had been coursing through his veins since he'd talked to Olena, looking for Mahina, was still there and every time it ran through his heart it just seemed to ratchet up the anxiety he had coursing through his body.

The light from Olena's headlights was just enough to get him back to the ditch. He didn't want the heavy goggles on his face, no matter how much help it would be to see her.

He didn't want anything between them and he had a feeling she felt the same way.

"Mahina? Baby."

He heard the impact of her feet on the ground between them and by the time he heard her make a noise she was close enough for him to pick up and wrap his arms around her.

130

But if he did, he wouldn't be able to put her down again, so he held back.

The adrenaline of the capture was wearing off and damn it, it peeled back the layers of his need.

He wanted her.

More than ever.

MAHINA DIDN'T KNOW what to think. There was just a kind of surreal quality of the air around them.

How much time had elapsed since Baron had arrived on the scene, she didn't know, but the time that had passed was meaningful.

Just his touch made her whole spirit sing.

The way he looked at her made her feel like she was seen. Well, and truly seen.

Plenty of people looked at her, but the way Baron looked at her heated her blood, sent chills up her spine, and made other parts of her tingle in anticipation.

"I heard the shot."

"I had to prove that I meant what I said."

She nodded her head. What else could she do? "I don't know what I would have done if you hadn't come by."

"Yeah, you do." He gently took hold of her chin and lifted it so she could look him straight in the eye. "You would have let them go and stayed safe."

"A lot of good that would have done!"

"No," he shook his head. "It would have a lot. Proving that you're right."

She winced. That wasn't the point, not really. "I just wanted to get proof that there was something going on."

"And you've got it."

"Thanks to you," she reached out to touch his face, but he stepped back and away from her searching hand.

"Olena and Cullen are here."

She jumped a little at his words. "They are?"

He put his hand on her lower-back and reached down with his free hand for her backpack. "Let's go and see them. Show them that you're alive and well before Olena kicks me in the balls."

His words made her chuckle, but Mahina leaned back and looked at him. "And then?"

She could barely see him, just the highlights created by the headlights in the distance showed him the outline of his features, but that didn't explain the shiver that tickled up her spine. It was almost as if she felt his gaze on her body and the air between them crackled with electricity.

"And then," he ran a hand down her back and when it reached her lower back, he tugged her closer so she could feel the hard lines of his body and the heavy press of his erection, stealing what was left of her breath, "you're coming home with me."

THIRTEEN

Walking into Baron's house at the base was surreal for her. Just a few weeks ago she'd been left there, watching him leave for... wherever. And now, she was back again with him.

She'd felt his arousal earlier, so she had a hope that they might be able to finish what they started a few weeks ago, but she wasn't sure she had the energy for it.

Her whole body ached and her mind drifted back to her conversation with her aunt Lynn. When they'd spoken with Olena and Cullen, they both urged her to go with Baron to Schofield. It was closer and Olena's look of concern nearly tipped the scale, but Mahina didn't want to leave her mother at the Yoshino house yet again.

It was only a call from Lynn, who talked about how much fun her mother was having playing Scrabble and Hanafura that got her to agree to go to Baron's house.

Laid out on Baron's bed, she listened as he turned on the water in the shower.

She was exhausted, her whole body aching, and her limbs were heavy, but she just couldn't go to sleep.

Mahina had already told Baron to use the shower first.

She had been sure that the instant she laid her head down, she would be out like a light.

But she wasn't.

Once she put her head down, all she could think about was him.

The bedsheets under her cheek, the wedge of light shining from the crack of space between the bathroom door and the frame.

It drew her attention there.

Inside.

The sputter of water from the shower, the groan of the pipes caught her attention and held it.

Closing her eyes, she tried once more to fall into a restful slumber, but realized that she wasn't going to get it.

It wasn't the light, or the sounds, from the bathroom that was keeping her awake.

It was the images in her head.

She wasn't going to get any sleep without seeing for herself if her imagination came anywhere near the reality.

Mahina sat up, dropped her legs over the edge of the bed and stood, amazed that her legs didn't give out on the first step. Or maybe her legs were just as curious as the rest of her body.

The door swung open with just a touch of her fingers and the heat inside felt like a hot day in the summer months. Hot and humid, kissing her skin with moisture as if she'd just worked up a sweat.

Baron's back was to her as he stood in the shower, but the view didn't disappoint.

Mahina loved museums and fine art, poring over the works of art created by masters who spend their lives developing their skill and creativity.

If she had come upon a sculpture of the male form in a museum that looked like him, she would have been hard pressed to leave that particular gallery in favor of any other. Every minute movement changed the shape of his body. Muscles bunching and stretching under skin, the uninterrupted tan and the drops of water coursing down his back, it was all a masterpiece of the human form.

And there she was, just a few feet away.

Incredible.

"You going to stand there?" He turned his head and gave her a glance over his powerful shoulder. "Or... are you coming inside so I can see just how slippery I can get you?"

Mahina's shoulders twitched with laughter, but the humor didn't do a thing to extinguish the heat of arousal that she felt traveling over every inch of her skin.

"I think I'm going to go crazy if we're interrupted again."

She moved away from the door and reached up for the elastic band in her hair.

"Leave that, baby. I'll take your hair down."

Mahina had no idea why every simple phrase that came out of his mouth had the same reaction as his mouth on her skin.

Just hearing his words, delivered on a harsh half-whisper, made her feel wide awake and needy.

Mahina dropped her hands to the hem of her top and lifted it up, shaking her head as the neck opening of the shirt threatened to catch her hair and tug it painfully.

She turned and dropped it on top of the hamper before reaching around for the hook on her bra.

"Leave that for now, 'Hina. Take off your pants first."

Smiling at him, she shook her head and opened the front of her pants, and shoved the black denim jeans off of her hips, including her panties with it.

"I was hoping you'd take those off separately."

Mahina looked up at him with a smile. "If you want a stripper, you can-"

"I want you. Come in here."

He opened the glass door and held it open for her.

As she stepped into the shower, she unhooked her bra and dropped the dark cotton onto the tile. The only conscious thoughts in her head were how much she wanted to be with him and how little she knew about seduction. She prayed that she wasn't about to embarrass herself.

"Stop thinking so hard."

Mahina felt his hand on her waist, hot and wet from the shower. "Is this too hot?"

She looked up at him and saw the intensity in his gaze. "Not yet," she blew out a breath, "but I have a feeling it's going to get there."

His smile sent shivers down her spine and she wondered why the drops of water falling around them didn't turn to steam.

She lifted her hands and set them on his chest, marveling in the difference of her skin against his. Ivory against tan. Fanning her fingers against his chest, she leaned in and rose on the tips of her toes to offer him a kiss.

And he gave it to her.

Water coursing off of his shoulders flowed around her like a waterfall, caressing the skin it touched as his lips worked against hers.

He raised a hand to the nape of her neck and his fingers grasped her hair tie and slowly worked it down to the ends of her hair. The tie caught on her hair and the way it tugged on her scalp, it made her gasp.

His tongue swept into her mouth, rubbing against her own.

The friction sent shivers through her body, her nipples tightening and tingling as her fingertips bit into his chest. He drew back, looking down into her eyes. "I missed you while I was gone."

Her hands relaxed against his chest as heat bloomed between her legs. "I missed you too." She felt the heat prickling against her cheeks. "I... I dreamed of you."

He dove in for another kiss, eating at her lips until she sagged against him.

There was no mistaking the heavy press of his erection against her belly and she arched her back to get even closer to him.

Her knees buckled and she heard the heavy slap of his face towel as it hit the tile.

Baron slanted a kiss over her mouth and wrapped his arm around behind her thighs.

"Oh," she tensed as he lifted her feet off the tiles, "Baron."

He nipped at her bottom lip and pulled back.

Meeting her startled eyes with his hard stare.

Mahina had no idea what she'd done to make him stop, she just wanted to fix it. She wanted him so much.

"Malcolm."

She shook herself to clear her thoughts and focus in on him. "Sorry?"

"Malcolm. That's my name."

She licked her lips and his gaze fixed on her mouth.

"Say it." His voice was rough, jagged. The look in his eyes was wild and demanding. "Say my name."

"M-malcolm."

The change in his face was almost too minute for her to see it, but she felt the change in his body the most. He lowered her to the ground, the water slipping between them adding to the delicious sensations of skin on skin. The flex of his muscles under her hands and the hard pulse of his cock against her belly.

Encouraged by his reaction, she moved her hands up his chest, up along the sides of his neck, and to the sides of his face.

Mahina felt a muscle tick in his jaw and she saw for the first time in his face, and his eyes, a kind of vulnerability that she didn't think many people had ever seen.

Something about this big, god-like man showing her the man behind the glare made her feel powerful and sexy.

Holding onto his face, she arched her back, dragging the hardened tips of her breast against his chest.

He groaned and when she raised herself up onto her toes, she sucked in a breath. The friction of her sensitive nipples against his chest and the bite of his fingertips into the underside of her butt pressed her body against his. The water that squeezed out from the space between them made her feel like they were sealed together, fused in a way.

She smiled and tugged at him, bringing his face closer to hers. "Malcolm."

He shook his head a little and the barest hint of a smile touched his lips. "I never should have told you."

"Oh yes, you should." She stretched up on her toes and pressed a kiss to the underside of his chin. "Malcolm."

He growled under his breath and it sounded more like a wildcat purring.

He liked that.

Mahina pulled him closer and pressed a kiss to his jaw, climbing up higher along the hard ridge until her lips brushed against the lobe of his ear.

He groaned and she closed her lips over the same spot, drawing her tongue along the sensitive spot.

"Fuuuck, baby."

She smiled and that tug on his skin made him shudder against her.

Mahina felt, for the very first time in her life, as if she had power. Malcolm had given that to her.

She used her teeth on his skin and his hands gripped her,

almost painfully, as he ground his hips against her own, hissing through his teeth.

"Fuck me..."

"If you're asking," she felt her heart pounding in her chest, adrenaline rushing through her veins, "then yes."

"Don't joke, baby. I want to get inside you." He kept his hands on her and dragged her onto his leg, her legs straddling his thigh. "Fuck, I need to get inside you."

"Then do it, Mal. I need you just as much."

"MAL."

She called him Mal.

And fuck, he'd never been so hard.

Even with the water coursing over their bodies, he felt the sticky slide of pre-cum between their bodies. Baron felt a kind of perverse satisfaction, marking her like that, but he needed more.

He reached behind him and turned off the water and before she had a chance to argue with him, he leaned over and picked her up on his shoulder.

"Mal!" Her hands fell on his back as he pushed the shower door open.

She laughed and it didn't kill the mood. In fact, it made him smile, too.

The fire he felt inside didn't dim, it grew hotter and higher.

And when he got to the side of his bed, he dropped her down on the surface, making her bounce a little higher toward the headboard. He didn't waste a single moment climbing up on the bed, crawling after her.

The look on her face threatened to break him.

Her naked hunger was mixed with an expression he didn't want to name.

He wanted to, but he knew his heart couldn't take it. It was brittle enough as it was.

And emotions... they were dangerous for a guy like him. He had no problem making a woman scream and lose herself over and over, but he'd never cared about feelings.

That wasn't the point of sex.

He couldn't change things now.

It wasn't possible.

He wasn't that kind of guy.

Baron gave himself a mental kick. He'd struggle with his thoughts later, right now, he had a woman to pleasure and adrenaline to wear off.

He needed this.

You need her.

He knew he couldn't stop the thoughts in his head, but he could drown them out.

He pushed in between her legs, his hands on her knees, his gaze fixed on her face.

Mahina looked startled, but she didn't fight him or pull away. Instead, her thighs relaxed and she opened for him.

She was fucking glorious.

Smiling, he reached out and opened the draw next to his bed, pulling out a box of condoms.

She blushed as he leaned over her. "That's a big box."

"I've got big plans." He opened it up and pulled out a single packet. "We'll start with one."

Mahina swallowed and he watched her throat work as he sat back, tearing the packet open with his teeth. His gaze moved over her body from her throat, over her perfect breasts and down over her softly rounded belly.

"I want to taste you all over." He fixed his gaze on her sex, bared to his gaze. "But I want inside you even more."

She groaned and Mahina covered her face with her hands. "Stop talking about it and do it." Mahina shook her head. "Please, just... So many times I dreamed of you and..."

"And what, baby?"

She shook her head, keeping her hands over her face. "Baron, I-"

He held the condom between his fingers and leaned forward, sliding the shaft of his cock against her clit before pulling away.

She stiffened at the contact and her hands dropped away from her face. "W-Why did you stop?"

He gave her a hard look and then a smile. "Malcolm."

She rolled her eyes and glared at him. "Really?"

Baron grinned, almost laughing at her outrage. "I just want to hear you call me by my name."

"Okay, Mal."

Fuck. He liked the way it sounded.

Smiling, he leaned over her body and took her lips in a kiss.

She grabbed the back of his head with one hand and the back of his neck with the other. "You like that," she breathed when he lifted his lips from hers.

"Damn straight, I like that."

She smiled up at him, her eyelids lowering a little. "Good to know, *Mal*."

"And you like torturing me." He kissed her again and they ended up laughing and kissing at the same time.

How?

Well he had no fucking idea and it didn't matter, really.

No use in trying to figure out how they were doing what they were doing. He just kept doing it.

And she had her hands all over him. Neck. Shoulders. Chest.

When she turned her head to catch a breath, he pressed a kiss against her neck.

"Well, you're driving me crazy when you do that."

"Do what?" He rubbed his cheek against her throat, knowing that he had a bit of scruff on his cheek. "This?"

When he moved back, he winced. He'd left behind some of the paint he'd worn along her neck. "I thought I washed all of that off."

She laughed and reached out to him. "You can wash it off of me later."

"You're going to drive me crazy," he shook his head at her and when he leaned in to kiss her again, he reached his hand between them and smoothed the condom over his dick. "You're going to feel so damn good."

She kissed him when he leaned closer and smiled. "I already feel good, Mal. I need more."

He saw the pink on her cheeks and the way she turned her head slightly to hide her expression from him.

She wasn't used to talking like this.

Good.

He didn't want to think about another guy while they were together.

Baron slipped his fingers between them and dragged the tips of two of them between her folds.

Shit. She was wet.

Slick. And hot.

Turning his hand slightly, he slipped one finger into her sex and smiled when she moaned. When he slipped another finger in beside the first, she arched her back, lifting her against him.

"Like that?"

He knew she did, but he had to ask.

A man likes to know when he was doing a good job.

Her thighs spread open farther and that let him get closer

to her, let him twist his hand and when he plunged those fingers back inside of her body, his thumb brushed over her clit.

"Mal," her lips parted on a moan, "just like that."

Again, he worked his fingers inside her and his thumb against her clit.

Mahina's soft moans and the gentle lift of her hips brought her in contact with the hard length of his erection and he found himself rocking his hips along with hers.

"Mal," she reached a hand up to his shoulder and dug her fingers in, "stop playing."

"That's not playing, 'Hina. Not by a long shot."

"Mal, please."

Maybe it was the look in her eyes, bright and shining.

Or maybe it was the sound of her voice, deeper than usual, sexier.

Or maybe it was the way the walls of her sex gripped his fingers and squeezed, making the blood drain out of his head and into his cock.

Fuck! Maybe it was all of it, but Baron knew one thing for certain.

He had to get inside of her.

Now.

He slipped his fingers free and with his other hand splayed across her lower back, he wrapped his hand around the root of his cock and fit it against her slick folds.

He managed to hold it together as the head of his cock slipped inside of her. There was no way to explain it, but that simple touch, the way her body wrapped around his, felt like an embrace.

Baron looked at her, carefully watching her expression for any sign of pain or discomfort, but all he saw was the way her eyes widened and then he felt her hips rise to meet him.

He hadn't planned it, but with that one simple movement, he sank into her body.

It wasn't an easy fit, but it happened, her body stretching around his and taking him in as if it was as simple as gravity.

Mahina opened her mouth to speak, but he didn't hear a word.

He saw her shake her head in disbelief, but he didn't ask her about it. His heart was in his throat, cutting off his air.

Baron put his hands on her hips and held her steady as he moved against her. A subtle grind, a lifting curl of his abs, moved him closer, impossibly deeper.

He closed his eyes for a moment, reveling in the way he felt with her pussy stretched around his dick.

This, he knew, this is what was going to get him in trouble.

It wasn't just the heat of her body around him or the soft keening cry when he pulled out, almost to the tip, it was also the way her body held onto him as if she couldn't bear for him to leave.

It was also the way her hands moved over his skin, as if she was searching for something only to settle on his shoulders or his forearms and dig into his skin.

Mahina was wickedly smart, he knew that for a fact, but she was also trying to get close to him. Laying herself bare before him in a number of ways.

He hated himself for doing this, but he couldn't quite make himself stop.

He knew he'd never hurt her, not intentionally, but he also couldn't stay away from her physically. He couldn't seem to make himself stay away and she wasn't pushing him away, either.

"More, Mal... please."

Fuck. There was no way he could walk away from this... not yet.

"Mal-"

He shifted slightly to the side and reached his hand around her thigh. Lifting it up, he brought it close to his side and felt the sudden stop as he bottomed out inside of her.

Mahina's eyes widened in shock and then she met his concerned gaze with her a smile.

"Yes," her hips rose to meet him as he thrust into her again, "like that."

"Well, if that's what you want, princess. Then that's what you'll get." And he set about giving her exactly what she wanted.

FOURTEEN

Baron woke up to an odd beeping sound. It wasn't the fire alarm in his home, that had a piercing sound, something shrill that stabbed into his ear.

The sound that had startled him awake was a musical refrain that sounded like a cell phone ringer.

He didn't know the song, but he could still hear it.

Something with a decent amount of bass to it, but still, he couldn't place the song at all.

"Babe." He swallowed and yawned before shaking Mahina's shoulder gently. "Baby. Is that your phone?"

"Hmm?"

He didn't think she heard him and he watched her turn onto her stomach and pull a blanket up over her head. "'s not Monday."

"No, baby, it's not, but I think your phone is ringing."

She burrowed deeper under the blanket and he reached over her to look for the phone.

It wasn't on the nightstand on her side of the bed, but he could hear the song better there.

Pushing the sheet off of his body, he moved to the bottom of the bed and got up. Fighting off a yawn, he bent down and reached under the bed.

As soon as he got his hand around the phone, he felt the buzzing sensation against his palm, and then the music started again.

Fuck.

Baron got up and sat on the edge of the bed before he turned the phone over to see the screen.

"Olena's calling you."

He held the phone out to her and saw Mahina crack open an eye a moment before she reached out her hand.

"Who? Olena?"

"Yeah. She's calling you. Why-"

She shot upright in bed, shoving her hair back from her face so she could see the screen. The call went to messaging and she hit redial, putting it on speaker.

Olena picked up the call a moment later.

"Mahina! I'm sorry to bother you-"

"What's wrong with my mom?" Mahina started toward the bathroom and Baron was on her heels.

When she paused just inside the doorway, he moved past her to pick up her clothes.

"She's sick. We don't know exactly what's going on but my mom called 911."

"Okay, are they there yet?"

Baron held out her panties so she could step into them. One leg went in before she put her hand on his shoulder to steady herself and then she slipped her other leg in.

"Fire is pulling up now."

Mahina nodded, but Baron was pretty sure she didn't have any idea what she was doing beyond listening to her friend on the phone.

He picked up her pants and helped her put them on too.

"I'm going to head out as soon as I can. I think I can get a Lyft on base."

"What?" Olena's voice was tight and thin.

"You're not getting a Lyft." Baron had to hold back the angry snarl in his voice as he turned her around and zippered up the front of her pants. "I'm taking you where you need to go."

"Baron, stop."

He leaned in and stared into her eyes as Olena's voice came through the phone. "Let Baron drive, you're in no condition to drive."

He moved away a few steps and came back with her bra. "Sorry, babe, it's a little wet."

"Baron, stop. I can do that."

"I'll let that one slide, Hina. But let me help you get dressed."

He could tell that she didn't think she needed his help.

He wondered if she felt like she had to reject his help to stand on her own two feet. Well, he'd give her a reality check later.

For the moment, he could feel the tension rolling off of her in waves, so he pulled her into his embrace and placed a kiss on the crown of her head. "Argue with me later, baby. Let's just get you to your mom, okay?"

She melted into his embrace, her cheek against his chest.

Nodding, she cuddled closer. "Okay. Okay."

"Mahina?"

She pulled away and turned her focus back to the phone. "Yes?"

"My mom is going to ask them to take her to Straub, okay?"

Baron felt her shiver and pulled a large bath sheet from a hook on the wall and wrapped it around her body to warm her up.

"Mahina?"

She tipped her head back and looked at the ceiling, blinking her eyes. "I heard... I heard you. I'm just..."

Baron combed his fingers through her hair, working his fingertips against her scalp.

"I'm just..." she sighed and dropped her chin to her chest while he continued to gently massage the nape of her neck, "I'm just worried."

Fuck him. He wanted to wrap her up in his arms and fend off the whole damn world.

He'd crawl over a sea of broken glass just to take that trembling tone from her voice.

"We'll be here with your mom. We're going to do every-thing we can to make sure she's okay."

"I'm... I'm so sorry I'm not there."

"Don't."

Baron heard the emotion in Olena's voice, too.

"Don't apologize. We've got this. We've got you, too."

Mahina squeezed her eyes shut. "Love you."

Olena's voice broke a little on the phone. "Love you, too."

Mahina clutched the phone like it was a lifeline. "Call if... if anything changes."

"You know I will. Now, drive safe."

Baron took the phone from her hands and ended the call before he set it aside. "I'll drive you. No need to bother with a Lyft."

She leaned back and looked up into his eyes. "You don't have to."

He smoothed his hands over her shoulders and gave her a gentle kiss. "I'm taking you to see your mom."

She gasped in a long, slow breath and gave him a watery smile. "Okay. Thank you."

He helped her on with her shirt , shaking his head. "There isn't much I wouldn't do for you, gorgeous. Now let's get going."

MAHINA FELT a world of guilt on her shoulders. As she sat by her mother's bedside, the doctors came in to explain what they'd found.

"An underlying infection in her bloodstream," the doctor explained in his quick, clipped tones. "You might have seen some changes in her demeanor."

Mahina shook her head and pressed her fingertips to her

temple. "I don't understand this. She was under her doctor's care."

The doctor drew a rolling stool over to the bedside and sat down beside her. "Looking at her records, I can see why her doctors made the diagnosis they did. Her symptoms checked all of the boxes."

"But you realized it was something different when..."

"It was a little hit and miss with bloodwork. With our elderly patients, it sometimes takes a bit of a hunt to find out which illness we're dealing with."

"Okay." Mahina leaned heavily on the arm of her chair. "But now that you know what it is, how soon can we bring her home?"

The doctor's lips pressed into a thin, pale line and Mahina drew in a deep breath through her nose, struggling to hold herself together.

"That's what I wanted to talk to you about, Miss Yoshino."

Miss Yoshino. She felt a chill descend along her spine. It felt like she was back in time talking to her mother's doctors during their first consultation and diagnosis. They gave her the same long look, too.

Dementia.

Alzheimer's.

Sundowning.

Vascular-

"We've placed your mother in a medically induced coma to give the medicine time to work through her blood and to give the cultures that we've started in the lab some time to speciate. Once we see final confirmation in the next few days, we'll make sure that we have the right diagnosis and go from there."

A few days.

Goodness.

That was going to be difficult. Seeing her laying there, a

151

machine measuring her breaths and other machines taking her vitals.

Mahina knew that her mother would come back out of this in her typical stubborn fashion.

"She'll be home in a few days." She gave the doctor a look that dared him to argue with her. "You've just met her and I know it's tough to look at her... to look at her where she is and think I'm not crazy.

"But my mom has been a force of nature all of her life. Even when everyone around her thought she would break, she was the one who kept her head held high and raised me.

"She'll come through this."

The doctor hesitated, and Mahina swore she could hear the tone of his thoughts. He was trying to figure out a way to tell her the bad news.

The last thing she wanted to do was argue with the man. He was the one who found out the real cause of her rapidly shifting moods. He didn't need a hassle from her. And she was exhausted.

"I'm sorry," she stood up from her chair and held out her hand to the doctor, "I hope you know that I appreciate your help. You've given my mother a chance to heal. That means the world to me."

He shook her hand and cast one last look at her mother's hospital bed. "Once we bring her out of the coma, we'll be able to see what lasting effects the infection has had."

Mahina gave him a smile and nodded. "She's too stubborn to let this get her down, doctor. You'll see when you meet her. My mother is going to surprise everyone."

He tucked his clipboard under his arm and gave her shoulder a pat. "Talking to you, I think you're right. Having raised a young woman like you, I can see how brave and stubborn she must be. Hold on to that thought, Miss

Yoshino. She can still beat this and she needs people she loves around her."

She nodded. "I'll be here with her."

He paused at the door, turning around. "That's what I like to hear."

WALKING out into the waiting room, Mahina drew up short. She'd expected Olena and her family to be there. Her family had been the closest thing she and her mother had to relatives all of these years.

But it was the sight of the waiting room filled up with Baron, Cullen, and the rest of the soldiers in their unit that surprised her.

And the women. They were there too.

Olena gave her a hug and when she stepped back, she took Mahina by the shoulders. "When they heard what happened to your mother, they all came to be here for you."

Mahina looked from one side of the room to the other and saw all of the men from Baron's unit. Ajax and his wife, Hi'ilani were the first couple she saw. Mahina moved over to them when Hi'ilani patted the empty seat beside her. She wasn't supposed to be on her feet much so Mahina was more than happy to sit beside her.

As soon as her butt hit the chair, Mahina groaned. "My legs are like noodles."

Hi'ilani took her hand and gave it a squeeze. "Mine will be too once this baby is born. Jack barely lets me walk past the end of the bed or further than the bathroom."

Mahani sighed at the picture in her head. "He loves you a lot."

Hi'ilani nodded. "I'm grateful to have him back in my life. And with him, all of the guys in the unit and women like you."

Women like me?

Before she could ask Hi'ilani what she meant, another of Baron's friends stepped up. The woman with him spoke first. "I'm glad Baron finally pulled his head out of his ass. I'm Tehani, and the big guy," she rubbed her hand over his belly, "is Boss. Devon Boseman."

Boss, wrapped a big arm around Tehani and pulled her against his side. "Tehani puts up with me."

Tehani leaned in and gave Mahina a kiss on the cheek. "I'm a flight attendant, so my schedule can be a bit up in the air, but if you need help with your mom after she goes home. Call me, okay?"

Mahina felt her jaw drop a little. "No. No, it's okay."

Tehani smiled at her. "Just think about it. I know we barely know each other, but we'll be there for you if you need it. You've got all of us now."

As they moved back, Mahina caught sight of Baron off to the side. He was leaning against the wall, his arms folded across his chest and his eyes on the scene between them.

She wasn't sure what the look in his eyes meant, but she knew the hard set of his jaw. He wasn't happy.

And Mahina had no idea why.

Before she could get up to talk to him, she met Train and his fiancée, Ku'uipo. Shado, his wife, Lilinoe, and their baby. The last group was at least partially familiar.

Mahina tried to stand up and greet Samira Chastain, but the other woman waved her back into the chair. Samira leaned closer and pressed a kiss on each cheek. "We left the kids at home since they have school."

"I didn't expect everyone to come to the hospital."

Samira gave her a soft, gentle smile. "You'll get used to it. I hope you know that you can call and ask for help whenever you need it."

She looked up at her husband, Anthony, who was the

senior officer in the unit and gave him a look. "Why don't you go check on Baron and see how we can help."

Anthony gave his wife a playful salute before he walked across the waiting room.

Samira's energy was calming and gentle, and Mahina took the hand that she offered.

"I wanted to thank you again for your help that day."

She shook her head in response. "No need to thank me, Mahina. From what Baron told Anthony, you'd never had him take off like that before."

"Actually," Mahina felt her cheeks heat, "I still don't understand what happened. Since Malcom and the others came back, there hasn't been a whole lot of time to talk. I feel like I'm up at the Pali Lookout and the wind is whipping around me. I don't know whether I'm coming or going really."

"I wish I could say things are going to be easier for you, but if there's one thing about being with these guys, it's never going to be a normal life in any way, shape, or form."

Mahina saw the way Samira was smiling and she just had to ask. "You don't seem..."

"Upset? Shocked?" Samira waved off the idea. "It's incredible, to say the least. Some of my friends told me I'd hate being married to a military guy, but they were wrong."

Mahina's eyes widened and she leaned back a few inches. Surely, Samira didn't quite understand what was going on between herself and Baron.

"Mal," she corrected herself.

Samira's expression was on the soft side of stunned. "I'm sorry, did you just call him-"

"Sorry, I'm just exhausted."

The glint in Samira's eyes shone brighter. "No need to worry about me or the others getting in your way, Mahina. Even though Baron can be a bit of challenge, we all love him and having you as part of our family... it's a good thing."

"Part of your family? I think you're mistaken. I'm not... I mean, we're not... like that."

Samira gently laid her hand over hers. "It's how we see it. It's not a bad thing, is it? Having some extra family around?"

Mahina felt like a bit of a fraud at her words.

She wasn't in any kind of real relationship with Mal, at least not that they'd said anything. Sex wasn't something you could build a relationship on. She'd seen romantic comedy movies like that, but that's what they were, movies. And Mal?

She couldn't see him in those movies either.

What they had... well, she didn't know what it was, but she wasn't about to argue with Samira. After Mal and the others in his unit had been called away, it was Samira, who lived on base with her husband, Anthony Chastain, who came over and explained why he'd run off so quickly.

But it was different for her, for the other women, they were in relationships. They knew that their men were coming back for them.

To them.

She had no idea if Baron would still be around her in a week or a month. She'd heard about him from Olena and Cullen. Nothing bad. It was obvious that he was a good guy under all of the snark and hard glares.

Mahina was under no misconception that he was interested in something long term.

She didn't have time for something like that anyway.

So, as long as she could have him, she'd do it. She doubted she'd ever find someone like him again.

"Hey."

Startled, she turned and saw Mal at her shoulder.

He gave her an endearing half-smile. "You want me to take you home?"

Mahina turned back to Samira and saw her wistful smile

directed at the both of them. She didn't want her to have the wrong idea. That would only make things harder on Mal.

Who knew when life would put a large wedge between them. She didn't want that, but there were a lot of things in her life that were likely to push between them.

Her wishes for more moments with him seemed so very selfish and greedy.

"Hina?"

She looked away and blinked repeatedly, trying to ease the prickling tears at the backs of her eyes. Then, with an indrawn breath she turned to him with a smile on her lips.

"The nurse is bringing me a cot so I can stay in the room with her. The doctor wants someone familiar in the room with her."

He looked like he needed a moment to process her words and then *he* was gone.

Mal was still physically standing there, but his eyes dulled and his lips tightened into a straight line.

"Yeah. Okay."

He took a slow breath into his lungs and walked away.

"Mahina?"

She swallowed and turned to look at Samira, trying to still the roiling feeling in her gut. Mahina didn't know what she could say to make the other woman understand what she was thinking, so she decided not to try.

Standing slowly, she pressed her palm against her belly and tried to give Samira a smile without meeting her eyes.

"I'm sorry. I really am. I just... I have to go and sit with my mother."

Samira reached for her, but Mahina turned to address the waiting room.

"Thank you, all. I... I can't tell you how much it means that you came, in the middle of the night, to be here with us. I am sorry to say that I have to go back into the room." Her feet shifted under her, squeaking lightly on the linoleum floor. "I'm sorry. I'm sorry, but I have to go."

She made it maybe ten feet before Olena caught up to her. "Hey."

Mahina refused to turn around. "I can't right now."

"I'm... I'm worried about you. This... this isn't like you."

"This is me." She looked over her shoulder but thankfully she wasn't able to meet Olena's gaze with her own. "I'm a mess. I'm a horrible person, an absent daughter. I know, Olena. I know all of my shortcomings. Okay? I know I owe you and your family so much, but right now... I feel like I have nothing to give."

It hurt to rip herself open like that, but she had no idea what else to do or say. It would be better to put some physical distance between them so she didn't damage their friendship anymore.

"Please, thank your mother for me. I'll... I'll do what I can to make it up to all of you once I pull myself together."

She didn't wait for a reaction. If she did, she might cave in and break down crying. She might even beg Mal to come back to the hospital.

It was so wrong, but she wanted him there. She wanted to hold him. To lay her head on his shoulder and feel his breath against her cheek. She wanted the comfort of his presence, but that was the problem.

Getting closer... being closer to him meant that the space she'd have to fill later when he walked away would be like the grand canyon instead of the heart-sized hole that she felt in her chest.

"You know we love you, Mahina." Olena's voice was far kinder than she deserved. "We love you no matter what. Remember that."

She tried to nod, but ended up shaking her head from side to side.

"Call and talk to me-"

"If I need you, right."

"No. Anytime. Call and talk anytime."

With tears coursing down her cheeks, Mahina walked away.

FIFTEEN

It was still dark outside when Mahina woke up. She'd only asked for a cot after she returned to her mother's room and there wasn't one available, but a nurse had brought in a second arm chair in from a room down the hall and by pairing them together, Mahina had managed a kind of restful sleep for a few hours.

When the nurse went through the morning rounds, taking note of her mother's vital signs, Mahina watched silently from the side.

She wasn't used to seeing her mother like this.

It was one thing to see her demeanor change at home, but there, they were moving around each other, or her mother was walling herself away in her room. There was a kind of frenetic energy that lived in the house with them, so it made it easier for Mahina to just cohabitate and not think beyond what they were being told.

Listening to the doctor, who had come back later in the wee hours of the morning, her mother's moods and her penchant for biting words and caustic comments might have been caused by the infection. Something more insidious than a UTI.

It had been an underlying illness, chipping away at her health from someplace no one could see.

A wound festering was one thing.

She could have seen that. It would have been noticed.

But what they'd finally diagnosed her with had been masquerading as an accelerating version of dementia. That didn't mean that dementia hadn't played a part, but her doctor had hope that once they beat back the infection she might actually regain some of her gentler characteristics. She might be more of the woman who'd she'd worshiped for her entire life.

The doctor's revelations also made her feel worse about her own feelings. Knowing now, what she didn't know then, the frustrations that she'd struggled with had stemmed from her mother's cold comments and her changing personality made her feel even more embarrassed.

Could she have done something more to help?

What had she missed because her own feelings had been stung by her mother's actions and words?

Mahina didn't know what to do to make things better, but she knew she had to try.

"Miss?"

Mahina turned and saw the nurse standing in the doorway.

Wiping at her cheeks, Mahina stood up and tried to paste a smile on her lips. "Yes?"

The nurse hesitated, her teeth biting into her bottom lip. "The finance office would like you to see them when you have a moment."

Finance Office.

This couldn't get any worse. Could it?

"Is that near the lobby?"

"There are directions from the lobby on the signs, or I can try to write down directions-"

"No, I'll get there just fine. Thanks. Sorry."

The nurse nodded and walked off down the hall, her clipboard clutched to her chest. It wasn't easy to bring up a topic like that.

Mahina folded the blanket that they had leant her and set it on the back of the armchair before she moved to her mother's bedside.

Suzume Yoshino looked so much smaller lying in the hospital bed than she looked in her own.

Then again, her mother had used a twin bed for as long as Mahina could remember, making her bed look smaller than it probably was in a comparative way.

Pushing her hair back and straightening her clothes, Mahina left the room to find her way down to the financial services office.

She had a feeling that it was going to be bad news and with the way she felt, the way she'd left things with Malcolm and his friends, she might as well take her lumps from the finance office along with her other emotional bumps and bruises.

What more did she have left?

BEFORE SHE REACHED THE OFFICE, Mahina saw a man standing outside the door. He was leaned up against the wall with one foot crossed over the other, holding a folder in his hand.

The closer she got, the farther away she moved from him. Her plan was to move around him and almost enter the office from the other side of the hall.

And she almost did, but just before she reached the door, he stepped into her way.

Mahina couldn't stop in time, but when she leaned back she found herself in danger of falling.

She stopped short of that embarrassing option and a moment later, she felt his hand around her arm.

Startled, she tried to pull back from him. "Let go."

He shifted on his feet and took a step to the side, putting him fully in the doorway in front of her.

With a slow, deliberate movement, he lifted his hand from her arm and lowered it to his side. "I just didn't want you to fall."

"Well, thanks. I think." Shying away, she rubbed at her arm, keeping her eyes on him. "Now, if you don't mind, I have to go inside."

He didn't move and for a quick second, she felt like she might break down in tears.

Instead, she pushed the feeling aside and lifted her chin to stare right into his eyes. "Please move."

His answering expression was hard at first, his eyes narrowing at her.

Then a moment later, he almost smiled. "I believe you're Mahina Yoshino."

She drew back a little and it was her turn to narrow her eyes at him. "That's my name."

His smile nearly turned to laughter, and she didn't know how to react to that.

"Why do you know me?"

He held up the folder in his hand and she saw her mother's name on the tab, visible just above his thumb. "I want to help you with your mother's care."

Her brain almost short-circuited at his words. "Why?"

He laughed then. A soft chuckle. "Why not?"

She turned her head to the side, giving him a hard side-eye look. "Why you? Why us? I can only guess that there are any number of people who are in need of care and the cost to pay it. I just don't know why you would concern yourself with my mother."

He shrugged. "Would it satisfy you if I said that I am a philanthropist with an interest in helping people?"

"Why aren't you just answering my question?" Her heart was pounding in her chest and her stomach was twisting in her gut. If he didn't start answering her questions with something other than a flippant answer, she was just going to push him out of the way and walk inside the office.

Maybe he saw that in her face.

Or maybe he just decided to make things easier on both of them.

Either way, it didn't matter, because he finally nodded and gestured to the room across the hall. "Perhaps," his smile softened and she didn't see any signs of laughter, "we could sit down and speak in private."

Mahina looked up at the plaque above the door.

CHAPEL

She nodded thinking that the room was close enough to the offices for someone to hear if things went sideways and while she didn't think money was the kind of conversation one had in a chapel, it would at least provide a calm atmosphere that might help her anxiety.

She slipped in through the doorway and took a seat on the first pew in the room, in full view of the hallway and offices.

He nodded and sat a few feet away on the same bench and laid the folder on the seat beside him.

"I received an application that you filled out."

Oh. She sat up straighter on the pew. "You did? I hadn't heard from any of the applications so I thought they were just thrown away."

"THROWN AWAY?" Sato shook his head and smiled.

The relief on Mahina's face was plain to see.

He liked seeing the effect he had on his daughter.

Without a smile, Mahina was beautiful. With a smile, she was like an angel. Ethereal and transcendent.

He couldn't wait to start their lives together.

"I am sorry about the wait, Miss Yoshino, but I had business matters that required my urgent attention."

She nodded. "I hope everything is better now."

His lips tightened a little as he recalled that the problem he'd encountered was because of his own daughter.

"It was a setback, but I have had such setbacks before. I always find a way to make things right and better my business because of it."

She smiled at him, but it was a tentative expression. "I've had some problems at work too, but I fixed it. Well, actually, I'm not sure that it's fixed, but I stopped it temporarily. The rest isn't up to me."

Sato grinned. Mahina might have caused his men and their delivery to be confiscated by the police, she had done her job and done it well.

It was a pity that he was going to have her fired.

Having a job would keep her busy and he wanted the time with her.

"It sounds like you're well valued at your job."

She hesitated again.

"Is something wrong, Miss Yoshino?"

"Wrong? No. I didn't listen to one of my bosses. I did something that I knew was right, but I didn't ask ahead of time."

He nodded. She'd answered one of his questions about the night that his delivery was taken.

He might have to believe Milton after all.

"Well, if you're valued there, they shouldn't give you too much of a problem as long as the situation worked out."

She grimaced and her fingers plucked at her pants leg in a nervous gesture.

He blamed Suzume for that.

She should have taught their daughter how to be calm and collected. This kind of nervous gesture would have to be fixed.

"I think I'll probably be written up, but I did what I believed had to be done. And I wasn't going to get personally involved that night, but Baron. I mean, Mal was there and he wasn't going to sit back and let it happen."

"This... Mal?" He managed a half-hearted smile, "is he a friend?"

"Friend?"

She was startled by the question and before he could take it back, he saw her blush and her eyes darkened.

This Mal was more than a friend.

Sato bit into the inside of his cheek and tasted blood.

"Anyway," her hand waved and she gave him a soft chuckle of her own, "you wanted to talk about my mother's care?"

He was grateful for the distraction. He knew that he would set some of his men on the task to find out who this man was and just how to get him out of Mahina's life.

"The waiver you signed in the financial aid package gave me permission to speak to the doctors about her care."

The look of concern that he gave her was an authentic one. He was upset by Suzume's illness and he was planning on having a... *conversation* with the doctor that missed the diagnosis.

Until then, he had other things to work out.

"The doctor knows that your mother's care will be paid for by my foundation."

"Which foundation?"

He smiled. "I'll give you all the details later when you sign the contracts as your mother's representative."

She shook her head. "I'm sorry. I interrupted you. I know it's not an excuse but I'm exhausted."

He nodded, happy to hear her apology. "Well, I'm hoping that our help will make things easier on you and your mother during her recovery."

She nodded and sat against the back of the pew, quietly waiting for him to continue.

Obedient. Or at least pliant when she needed to be.

Interesting.

"Her doctor warned me that she will likely need round-the-clock care when she is released from the hospital."

While she didn't say a word, Sato saw the change in her demeanor and her posture.

He could tell that his words weren't all that surprising to her, but she was still disappointed to hear them.

The doctor likely hadn't wanted to upset her.

"I thought since they found out what was making her sick that she'd be okay."

He heard the hesitation in her voice. Mahina was probably hoping for the best outcome.

"You really love your mother."

"Of course I love her." She narrowed her eyes at him. "Why wouldn't I?"

He narrowed his eyes at her and saw the hint of guilt in her expression. "The doctor explained that your mother's illness was changing her personality. Is that what happened?"

She hesitated and he saw the way her eyes filled up with tears. "I felt like I didn't know her anymore. She'd become dismissive at times and mean at others. I didn't know what to think anymore. It felt like I was losing her." She pursed her lips and shook her head as she looked down at her hands.

When she looked up at him again, he couldn't deny the pain he saw in her dark eyes. "Have you ever lost someone... when they weren't dead? It's like you're there in the room with them, but you can't be with them?"

It was as if she knew how he felt, sitting there, just a few feet from her.

"Yes." His single word sounded gruff and strained, but he could not tell her the truth.

Not yet.

She smiled at him, nodding her head. "I can hear it in your voice."

"My foundation is ready to offer your mother a fully paid residence at our care home."

"At a care home."

He held up his hands for a moment of time. "We're converting a property in Waialae-Kahala. The home is beach-front property with a pool for exercise and the best in security. Your mother will be protected and well cared for day in and day out."

"And we don't have to pay for this?"

He couldn't say that he was surprised at her answer. From all of the research he'd had his men do into Mahina's life, his father hadn't provided for them well enough. They'd had to make do with much less than his father had promised that he'd given them.

He was sure once he talked to Suzume, he would hear a lot about where his father fell short.

Where he fell short.

He should have known that his father wouldn't follow through with his promises.

"No, Miss Yoshino. There is no cost for this. When I read your statement about your mother I felt like I knew her."

"Really?" She smiled at him. "I'm so glad, I never liked writing essays in school."

"Your mother and I share a bit of our background as well."

"You do? What?"

He liked the eagerness in her tone and the light of joy in her eyes. He wanted to see that more.

"We're both from Kumamoto Ken. Your mother's ancestors came from there and it's where I was born. I like to think we share that and likely more. As she recovers I would be interested in seeing how much more we share."

"Oh, you're going to be there?"

"It is a property that I own and my foundation. I would hope to be there as much as time allows." He fixed his gaze on her face, needing to see her reaction. "Would that be fine with you, Miss Yoshino?"

Her smile was easy and quick. "Please, call me Mahina."

"I'll have the papers drawn up to give to the hospital so that they know she has a place to go when she's ready to leave here." He held out his hand. "Thank you, Mahina."

"No, thank you, Mister..."

How he longed to tell her who and what he was, but he'd settle for a beginning.

"Sato." He nodded. "Please call me, Sato."

"Sato," she said his name in a soft, almost wistful tone of voice and he was thrown back into the past by how much her voice reminded him of her mother's for just a moment. "It's nice to meet you, Sato."

Yes.

It was a beginning.

SIXTEEN

Two Weeks Later

Baron woke up to someone pounding on his front door.

For a long moment, he laid still in his bed, willing them to go away.

When that didn't happen, he considered calling the MPs to come by and tell whoever it was to fuck off.

That wasn't going to happen.

Not because the MPOs wouldn't help him out, but because he wasn't a complete wimp.

Throwing back his blanket, Baron got out of the bed and walked out to the front door. He didn't look to see who was out there.

If they were going to destroy his sleep, he didn't care if they got an eyeful.

Leaning an elbow against the wall beside the door, Baron yanked the front door open.

"What?"

He expected a curse word or two, but the laughter...

The laughter got him.

Cracking open an eye, he glared at the sight outside of his door.

Most of the women looked away, but Tehani took a good long look. "Well," she elbowed Boss who was standing beside her, "why don't you ever greet me at home like this?"

Sighing, Boss clapped a hand on her shoulder. "Babe, don't make me kick his ass."

Baron took a step back and held out his arms. "Everyone get a good look?"

"Can we avoid it?" Olena pinched the bridge of her nose when he didn't say anything.

Baron did a full 360 turn, trying to ignore the pain in his head from the drinks he had before he fell half-asleep.

"Baron, put it away. Get some pants on so we can talk."

He stepped back from the door and walked toward the living room. "You can talk, but I'm not promising clothes."

He changed his mind and course corrected to the kitchen and opened the door to look for a beer.

There wasn't one.

Fuck.

Before he turned around, he saw Cullen standing in his way, a pair of boxer briefs dangling from his fingers. "Put it on."

Baron raised an eyebrow at the order and opened his mouth to talk back, but he heard the commander sigh.

"Do it, Baron."

He snatched the underwear from his friend's hand and stepped into it with a few pointed words mumbled under his breath.

When he was done, his couch and half of the floor nearby was filled with much of his team.

"It's a fucking Sunday. How do you people not have something to do?"

He saw the look of warning on the commander's face. "Baron-"

"We're here for you." Samira gave her husband's knee a squeeze, calming him.

Baron saw the gesture and wanted to kick something across the room.

"Well, I'm here, but unless we have some kind of training today that I'm missing, I'd like to be alone."

He didn't hear a word spoken in the room, but he saw all of the looks that his team and their women gave each other.

It made him even more upset.

"Seriously, I'll be fine when I have something to do. Until then, I just want to be left alone."

Cullen started in. "Baron, we just-"

"You're just butting in where you don't belong."

Train, of all people, tried his hand at it. "We want to help."

"Help." Baron pointed at the door. "There's the door. You can help yourself right out the way you came in."

"Ohhhkay." Samira got up from her seat and put her hand on the commander's shoulder. He, in turn, put his hand over hers.

The gesture was one that Baron had seen hundreds of times, but this time, it hurt. It felt worse than being shot and Baron had his share of experience with that sensation.

But he'd never felt it cut so deep, or bleed so freely.

"Fuck."

"You know, I think we came at this all wrong."

The room went silent and when Baron heard the door shut, he looked up, expecting to have his house all back to himself.

"Well, shit."

He was staring at a couch full of women.

"Baron," Samira looked him right in the eye and pointed at the armchair, "please have a seat."

He hesitated.

And then he just stood there.

Waiting.

Hoping that they'd just give up and leave.

He might be an asshole, but he didn't want to dump on the women. He wasn't that much of an asshole.

Or so he hoped.

"You might as well sit your ass down before I make you."

That was from Olena.

"You and what badge?"

He heard the coffee table scrape across the floor and Tehani murmuring to Olena to "Sit down. You can beat him up later."

Holding up his hands in surrender, he walked across the room and flopped into the armchair. "Well?"

Olena looked at Tehani and Samira. "I told you we should've picked up Hi'ilani. There's no way he would have pulled this crap in front of her."

"And Ajax would have ripped him apart for upsetting her."

"Hello?" He waved at them. "Sitting right here."

Samira was close enough that she touched his hand. "We know. We're just a little frustrated."

"Join the fucking club."

Baron had meant to grumble the words under his breath, but apparently, he was fucking up all sorts of things.

"What's going on?"

He looked up at Olena and stared back at her. "Nothing. Nothing is going on and I like it that way."

The women shared another look, and he huffed out a breath.

"Now you can go. Right?"

"We'll go when you pull your head out of your ass."

Tehani and Samira looked at each other as Olena glared at him like she would gladly carve him up like a side of beef.

Given the looks the other women were giving each other, he had a feeling that they'd planned out who was going to say what, but Olena didn't want to follow the program.

"Where the hell have you been?"

Baron gestured at the room they were sitting in. "If I'm not training with the guys then I'm here in my house."

"Hiding away."

"Maybe we should soften up the argument." Tehani reached out and touched Olena's arm, but Olena shrugged it off.

"Baron gets why I'm pushing so hard. He's said it himself. You can't just hit him over the head with something, you have to bludgeon him with it, and kick his ass while you're at it, too."

"I thought you cared," he heard the snarl in his voice and wished he could take it back. It was one thing to be pissy by himself. But as much shit as he gave her, Olena was a friend.

Probably more than the other women.

He cared about them.

He'd take a bullet for every single one of them, but he wasn't a friend. Olena was probably as close to him as he'd ever been with one of the guys.

She deserved better than his current behavior, but at the moment, *this* was all he had. Olena might forgive him, but he wasn't feeling all that forgiving for himself.

As he sat there trying to figure out how to fix yet another mess in his life, he saw Tehani and Olena whispering to each other.

He should have used that as his opportunity to get out of Dodge, but being the glutton for punishment that he was, he sat there and waited for one of the women to kick his ass and put him out of his misery.

Instead, Tehani and Samira walked out of his house and left him alone with Olena.

"Should I ask you if you're armed?" Baron gave Olena a hesitant look.

"I have two of them, one on my right and-"

"One on your left." He shook his head. "You had to go and copy my joke."

"Jokes that bad," she smiled, "shouldn't be said at all, but I'm just making you suffer right along with me."

He nodded and realized that much of the bluster he'd been using to hold them at bay had bled out, leaving him exhausted and more than a little embarrassed.

"What do you want from me, Olena?"

She leaned on the arm of the sofa. "I'm trying to find out what's going on with you. You act like you're just fine, but you have to know that everyone around you, everyone who cares about you, knows that you're full of shit."

He tried to put up a front and laugh it off. "You kiss Cullen with that mouth?"

She pointed at her mouth and deadpanned, "I do a lot of things to him with this mouth."

He coughed out a laugh.

"Is that it? You're just frustrated? Or did you do something that pissed off Mahina? What's going on?"

"Like I said," his jaw was starting to hurt from biting off his words, "nothing. And it's better this way."

"Baron-"

"No, it is better. Look, we both know that I'm a complete and total shitshow of a person. I'm good at two things: kicking ass and having the backs of my team."

"Don't."

"Don't what? Tell you the ugly truth?" He felt a muscle in his cheek tense up. "Maybe that's what you need to hear. I'm not a guy that any woman should be with for longer than a night. I'm good for a long, hard fuck. But doing the rest of it?

The... the... talking part of it. The gentle part of it. The kindness part? I'm not that kind of guy.

"I'm handy with a gun. She had a problem at work. I dealt with it. You had them put in cuffs." He brushed his hands together. "Cleaned up. Done. And then we had some fun before her mom ended up in the hospital. You didn't have to see her face. The guilt. The anger-"

"She wasn't angry at you."

"The fuck she wasn't! And really, that was the best thing for her." He leaned back in the armchair and stared up at the ceiling. "She could barely stand to look at me. And that's a lesson she should remember. Being with me isn't what someone like her should do. I'm that kind of embarrassing mother fucker that makes it hard for someone good like her to look in the mirror at herself.

"I bet she's relieved to put me in her rearview mirror. It's better if she keeps me there."

"Come on." Olena looked at him like she didn't know if she wanted to punch him or kick his ass. He would have been okay with both.

Physical pain, he'd discovered, was a damn sight better than this.

Emotional.

He sounded the word out in his head.

Emotional.

"I'm such an ass."

"Well, we know that, and we still love you."

He turned his head to glare at Olena. "This isn't a damn joke!"

"I know that! Do you think I'm joking with you or something?"

When he didn't speak, she shook her head and glared at him.

"Boy, you really are a stubborn asshole."

He shrugged, almost smiling at himself.

"Do you have any idea what it's been like for her?"

"How?" He sat forward in the chair and glared at her. "How the fuck am I supposed to know? We don't talk. She's got her job. She has her mom to take care of. And if she called me, I'd be disappointed in her. She's smarter than that."

Olena sat back on the couch and brought her knees up so she could hug them to her chest. Her gaze dropped down to the floor and she took a long, indrawn breath. "Wow, you really are an asshole."

Something about the way she said it hit him square in the chest. Center Mass.

Straight through his heart.

Aw fuck.

So he did have one.

That was news to him.

"I just want you to answer something for me before I go."

That seemed easy enough. He shrugged his shoulders. "Sure. Go ahead."

"What was she to you, Baron? A curiosity? Or was she just a warm, willing body to fuck?"

"Shut up." He clenched his teeth together so hard he felt like he might pull a muscle in his jaw. "Don't say that about her."

"Why? 'Cause it's true?" She shook her head. "If I thought for a real fucking moment that you were only after her for fuck buddy, I would have beat you to a bloody pulp."

"Then why didn't you?"

He knew he was poking the bear. Waving a whole damn red carpet at a bull. He knew how close Mahina and Olena were.

"Why?"

The look on Olena's face made him ache in his chest.

"Why didn't I beat your ass?"

Oh, fuck. She was about to cry.

He really was a complete asshole.

"I thought you actually cared for her."

He really was his father's son.

"I don't know why you don't see it, Baron. Maybe you can feel it. Can you? Can you remember what it was like to be with her? To... to hold her?"

That was exactly what he didn't want to remember.

He woke up at night, again and again, with an empty bed and an ache in his chest.

"I keep hoping that I'll forget, damn it. The last thing I want is to remember what I can't have."

That stopped Olena in her tracks.

She went from pissed off to stunned in heartbeat.

The change shocked him just as much.

He would rather she be upset. He could handle her anger. Disappointment hurt.

"Why do you think you can't have her?"

The fact that it wasn't obvious to Olena drove home the fact that he was really fucked up in the head.

"You never met my dad."

Her eyebrows raised. "The way you say that, I'm thinking that's a good thing."

"It is. You wouldn't have anything to do with me if you knew him."

"I doubt that."

He laughed at her answer. Not because he thought she was being silly. He was just glad she didn't know how much of an ass his father was.

"He's always made it really clear exactly what a woman is good for."

"And?"

"And what?" He held out his hands, wondering what else

she needed to hear. "Do you want a kind of guy like that to be with your best friend?"

"Of course not!"

He lifted up his hands to say, 'See?'

"But you're not like that, are you? You don't think like that about women."

"N... no."

"Right. So you're just choosing to be an ass."

"I'm choosing to keep her safe."

"You," she glared at him, "are so full of it."

"Olena-"

"You're a liar to yourself. And you're a coward."

He saw red and his hands gripped the arms of his armchair. "I am not a fucking coward."

She was almost smiling at him.

"I'm not."

Olena got up from the couch and gave him a hard look. "Then prove it. Go and see her."

SEVENTEEN

Mahina pulled her car into the driveway at the Kahala house and sat behind the wheel. It killed her to sit there, but she also relished the quiet and alone time that it gave her.

Over the last few weeks, her life had changed.

Her job at Kaena Point wasn't there anymore.

Even though they'd caught the men damaging the sensitive nesting areas, she'd been reassigned to the office in Downtown, Honolulu.

In a way, it was easier. Driving out to Kaena Point had always brought her close to Schofield Base and that was just a reminder of what she couldn't have.

Who she couldn't have.

Even her time with Olena had changed. That was by her own doing, really. It was just easier to text her friend instead of calling her. She certainly didn't have the time to see her. Between the office and her mother's care home, she didn't have a single moment to herself.

All Olena knew was that she was spending time with her mother and working hard. That, and she hadn't seen or talked to Baron since the morning her mother was taken to the hospital.

And every time Olena tried to talk about Baron, well, she just didn't have time to talk.

Yes, she was a horrible friend.

But she was trying to be a better daughter.

A good employee.

And today she'd come to the realization that she'd completely failed one of her two responsibilities.

At the end of her day, Milton had called her into his office and fired her.

Her 'Nancy Drew' stake out had opened their office and the non-profit to *bad press and governmental scrutiny*.

She tried to bring up the news stories that lauded her actions, but he had printouts of complaints to the office, including the threat of a lawsuit against her from the defendants.

Mahina was still ready to fight that, knowing that what she'd done had been in the interests of the refuge and the animals they were sworn to protect.

Then he'd dropped a bomb into her lap.

Those threats of lawsuits weren't just for her. They were going to include Malcolm, Olena, and her father.

As a captain with the Honolulu Police Department he could be accused in both the court and the court of public opinion as having used his position with the Police Department for personal gain.

How had she dragged these good people into trouble? Was she so selfish? Demanding? How could she have done this to her mother's lifelong friends and a man she'd just met?

As she sat in the driver's seat, she had to acknowledge that maybe there was truth in his accusations.

She had never intended to get anyone in trouble. Maybe

she'd excused herself by putting on blinders in what she felt was a good and just cause.

She knew that one part of her actions had been driven by her own personal need. Her personal desire. Malcolm.

Had she been so stupid in love that it had blinded her to the truth around her?

But if she admitted to that, or even posited it openly, she worried about his reaction.

He'd probably laugh if she said it to his face, but it was the truth.

They weren't even together as a couple. A date or two? A few hours in a roadside trench. It didn't seem like a romance to anyone.

Except to her.

She'd loved every minute.

Wanted more.

Wanted him.

But she couldn't have him.

She wasn't anything like the other women who got to love the men in his unit. She knew that there was something odd... No, something special about his unit, but she just wasn't like the others.

She wasn't talented like Hi'ilani. She wasn't the kind of woman who could kick ass like Olena. There was no way that she'd be the amazing mother and wife that Samira and Lilinoe were. She could go through and list everything she wasn't, but the most important thing she lacked was Malcolm.

And the empty ache she felt inside her chest made it hard to breathe.

Squeezing her eyes shut to hold back the tears, she reached out for her purse. She just wanted to hold her phone. She wasn't going to call him, she just wanted to-

KNOCK KNOCK

Startled, she turned in her seat and felt a chill go down her spine.

Sato. He was standing just outside her door.

Smiling at her.

Mahina struggled to breathe without gasping. He was a nice man. He did nice things.

There was just something... off when she looked at him. When he looked at her. It was as if he was... waiting for something from her.

She just had no clue what it was.

Lowering her window, she gave him as big of a smile as she was able. "Sato, hello. Is there something wrong?"

"I think I should be asking you," he explained. "You've been sitting out here for a few minutes. Is there something wrong? Something that happened at work?"

She didn't know what to say.

Her car door opened up and she sat staring at him.

"Come inside, Mahina. We'll talk over dinner."

"Uh, okay."

Picking up her purse she stepped out of the car, happy that he'd stepped back enough that she didn't have to walk directly by him.

The security guard at the door opened it up and nodded at her as she walked inside.

Her stomach twisted inside of her, and she realized that this home, where her mother was so well cared for, felt like a kind of prison.

Just a few steps in, she turned around and almost ran into Sato who had been standing silently behind her.

"Oh, sorry. I didn't know..."

He turned his head a little and leveled his gaze at her. He was never mean or even rude, but more and more, as the relief wore off, Mahina felt like Sato was watching her.

Waiting... for something.

Something she didn't understand.

"Is there something you need?"

His words were spoken in a mild tone of voice, but her physical reaction wasn't mild in any way.

Her pulse jumped up and her breaths shortened.

It was maddening to feel like she was supposed to 'know' what to do.

"Actually. I was hoping... I mean, I forgot that I agreed to go to my friend's house for dinner."

"Really? I don't recall that at all."

She forced herself to look him right in the eye. "I didn't think I had to clear my schedule with you."

His eyes narrowed at her, and she felt a cool sensation settle over her skin. "I would think that your mother's care would be foremost in your mind."

"Of course it is." She felt tears prickle at the backs of her eyes. "My friend and her mother have helped me care for her and Olena's mother is like a sister to her."

Something changed in his demeanor. His expression sharpened when she mentioned Olena's name.

"Then, we'll invite them over this weekend. They'll be able to see how well your mother is doing. And they can meet the doctor and nurses that are responsible for her care."

Mahina looked at the door behind him, but it was already closed, and she could see the silhouette of the security guard highlighted with the setting sun.

She was starting to realize that she was in a situation well over her head.

SUZUME WOKE UP to the sound of her daughter crying.

The room was dark but the shadows surrounding her didn't look like home.

The mattress under her was too soft. Too wide.

And her daughter was in distress.

Mahina.

Her mouth was moving, but she didn't hear any sound coming out.

Her daughter's tears and wracking sobs were too much for her to bear and Suzume reached out to find her daughter's hand.

But she felt nothing.

Again, she moved, but could only feel the cool sheet under her palm.

She couldn't move.

She couldn't speak.

That's when she heard the sounds beyond the crying.

The soft beeps droning on in a cacophony created different rhythms, like musicians out of sync with each other.

Mahina.

What was her daughter crying about?

Am I... am I dead?

Is that why Mahina was crying?

Her chance to get answers disappeared as sleep claimed her again.

WHEN BARON DROVE up to the Yasui house, he cursed under his breath.

Olena was standing outside with her arms folded across her chest and cheshire cat smile on her face.

"I'm going to regret this, aren't I?" He closed the Jeep door behind him.

"That's right, man." Cullen opened the door and stepped outside. "She's never going to let you forget that she had to light a fire under your ass to get you to make your move."

"I would have done it on my own."

Both of his friends looked at him with droll expressions.

"Eventually." Baron added the word, but even that didn't change their expressions. "I'm not that much of an idiot."

Olena rolled her eyes and gave him a wink. "Debatable."

"Look," Baron sighed, "can we verbally flog me later?"

Olena leaned in against Cullen and Baron had to bite back a jealous snarl. He'd been close to having that.

He knew it.

And he'd shut himself off because he'd felt himself getting that close to her.

He'd taken an odd moment between them and fucking blown it all out of fucking proportion, because... asshole.

"Hey," he felt Olena bump her hip against his side, "you okay?"

He shook his head. "No. Not in the least."

She smiled at him. "It's just who you are."

Baron raised an eyebrow at her. "Really? I thought you were going to put a hold on the flogging."

She gave him a wide-eyed 'naive' look. "When did I say that?"

He let out a sigh. "Have you ever felt like you knew everything that was going on around you... inside you... and then you find out that you're all wrong?"

"About everything?"

He nodded. "Yeah. About everything."

She thought about it for a moment and then shook her head. "No. I pretty much have my head on straight. I see things. I know things. It's part of the reason I wanted to put you guys together."

"Right."

Cullen cleared his throat and gestured into their house. "She's always right, Baron. Come in so we can draw up battle plans inside."

Baron looked at Olena and shook his head. "How much did you pay him to make him say that?"

Olena gave him another guileless expression. "Pay him? Nope." She walked toward the door and stopped to grab a handful of Cullen's ass. "I gave him the mother of all blowjobs."

Cullen's chin dropped down to his chest as his shoulders shook.

Baron paused beside his friend before he walked inside. "I don't need to hear about your sex life, man."

Cullen held up his hands in surrender. "If you were in my place, tell me that you wouldn't do whatever Mahina asked for the feel of her-"

Baron was suddenly staring up at his friend's face. He had both of his hands in the front of Cullen's shirt, lifting him a few inches from the ground and pressed against the wall beside the door.

"Don't," he glared at his friend. "Don't talk about her like that."

Baron lowered him back down to his feet and stepped into the interior of the house.

Olena was standing in the kitchen, staring at him wide-eyed.

"Wow." She actually smiled at him instead of shooting him. "You really are crazy, stupid in love."

Baron laughed at himself.

"I guess I am."

EIGHTEEN

A HERO FOR
MAHINA

MALCOM
ROTH
"BARON"

It began with a single twitch of her finger.

Suzume Yoshino felt herself rising up from the dark, as if she was floating up to the surface of the ocean. As a child, she'd gone swimming with her family in Japan. Her mother had been a pearl diver and thought her children would all be like her, swimming like fishes in the waters around her home country.

But Suzume was not a fish. Later, she would wonder if it was because her mother named her after a bird.

That day, as the others played in the ocean, Suzume found herself struggling to swim and then, as she sank below the surface, she found herself struggling to breathe.

Down.

Down.

Further down until her feet met the floor of the ocean near the beach.

Above her head, the light of the sun looked close enough, but she was so tired and her arms could barely move.

There was nothing to prevent her from dying on that day,

but as she felt the cool earth under her toes, a rush of warm water lifted her from the ocean floor.

Higher and higher until her head broke free of the water.

Rivulets and then drops of water coursed down over her skin and back into the water, but she had no idea why or how it happened.

There wasn't time to even think about it, because her mother was there, plucking her from the ocean and bringing her back to the beach.

That memory was with her now and again, she could not account for why she was slowly seeing the light before her.

It was not heaven, she did not believe that she would find her way there. She had been ill. She knew that, but she also had recollections, flashes of memory, of the things she had done. The horrible words she had said.

All happening as if she was sitting in the dark, watching it. Dreading it.

With no way to reach out and apologize.

And now, as her face felt the sun on it she gasped as if she had finally broken free of the water and was taking her first real breath of air.

"Suzume?"

That voice?

That voice!

"Sa-Sato?"

"Yes."

She turned her head slightly, for that was all she could do.

The man standing beside her bed reminded her of her Sato. He was older, like she was as well, but there was something missing from his face.

His expression.

He lacked the youthful light she remembered so well.

The easy smile that had turned her head in the first place.

"Suzume."

He took her hand and smiled.

She waited for that smile to strike a familiar chord in her, but it never happened.

The smile looked too tight and brittle to be her lover.

And a lover was all she had been.

His promise of love was what she held onto, but it had never come to pass. He never returned.

"I am... so glad to see you again."

The words should have made her happy, but all she could taste was bitter disappointment on the back of her tongue.

"It," she licked at her lips to moisten them, "it has been a lifetime."

She let her eyes fall closed before she startled and opened her eyes to stare at him before taking in the rest of the room. When she did, she met his eyes again and had to ask.

"Where am I?"

"You, Suzume*chan*. Are home. With me."

She could see the happiness in his eyes, but she knew that she could not share it with him.

"Wh-" She swallowed hard, trying to bring some moisture to her mouth. "Where?"

With a smile, he leaned closer to her and if she had been able to move, she would have flinched at the gesture.

She may have loved him once.

May have thought that their love would last forever.

That, she blinked away the tears, was destroyed when he left her alone.

"I have a house connected to the beach in Kahala. When you are well, we can swim in our pool or in the ocean."

She tried to shake her head, but she could barely move beyond a little wiggle.

How could he forget that she refused to get in the water?

"We can travel," he continued, "I can take you back to Japan now that we are together again."

She moved her head. "No... no."

"Not Japan?" He shrugged. "What about Spain? Or Italy?"

The more she moved, the more flexibility she had, but she slowed her movements down, wanting to keep that knowledge to herself.

She didn't understand the instinct at the moment, but now that she had more control over her body, she wanted to exercise it with caution.

So she kept mostly still.

"I don't want to go anywhere without my daughter." The weight of her love and the ache of missing Mahina seemed to descend upon her in a moment. "What have you done to her?"

When he answered her, there was a kind of feral fix to his smile. His eyes narrowed and yet they seemed sharper. So very different from the man she knew.

"Our daughter is having lunch with her... friend."

"Friend?" She felt an ache in her head that started at her forehead and was working around to the back. "Olena?"

"The police officer," he smiled, and she swore the temperature in the room dropped a few degrees, "yes."

"H-how do you know Olena?"

"There are things that you should not know. Things that are better left unsaid. I wouldn't want to make you fear me."

"F-fear you..."

She could only think of one reason why she might fear him in relation to Olena.

And the thought chilled her to the bone.

Olena had been captured, nearly killed. And one of Cullen's friends...

"When will she come back?"

He looked past her and into the hallway, nodding. When he sat back and took her hand, she refused to pull it away.

"I'll have one of my men bring her home. She'll want to see how well you are."

For a moment, she wondered if she had put her daughter in jeopardy. Sato had once been a sweet and gentle man, but she could see by the hard lines of his face and the cold cast of his eyes said that much had changed.

Suzume had dreamed of reuniting with him for years, but it was clear that the man who had returned to her was someone quite different from the man she loved.

The man she still loved.

There was no time for her to feel that loss. No time to mourn it.

The man at her bedside had a plan and until she knew what it was and made sure that he didn't hurt her daughter any more than she already had, she was going to keep him happy.

Turning her hand, she squeezed his fingers and she saw him smile.

"There's no rush, Sato."

His smile deepened and again, she was struck with how different he looked compared to her memories. "You rest, and when she returns, I will bring her to you."

MAHINA COULDN'T SEEM to eat much as she sat across from Olena. Her friend wasn't making things easy for her.

"I don't understand why you can't come home with me tonight."

"I thought I explained that I wasn't going to interrupt your time with Cullen."

Sitting back in her chair, Olena set her chopsticks down across her dish. "Just like this."

Mahina was shaken, not understanding what Olena meant. "Like what?"

Olena gestured at her. "You've been over... hundreds of times. You come over, we have a meal, watch something sappy on the TV while Cullen pretends to moan and groan and then we can stay up and talk or play games. Really, Ma-"

"This is exactly what I mean. You can't give up your time with Cullen." A muscle near her eye started to twitch so Mahina massaged her temple to try and stop it. "You never know what's going to happen. You can't just give away something so precious as time with him."

Olena, for once, seemed stunned into silence.

Mahina leaned closer to the table and braced her forearms against it.

"I'm not wishing for something to happen to him, I hope you know that. I'm just saying that there are times when you have to choose the best thing for your family and forget the rest.

"And Cullen, well, I know you love each other. So pretty soon, I'm betting he's going to drop down on one knee and ask you to marry him. You're going to want to have every single memory stored away."

Looking down at her plate, she saw the little pieces missing from her meal. The pieces that she'd swallowed down like marbles in her throat.

"I know that you kept secrets about Cullen's unit, but I know that if things were different you could tell me that secret. And that..." She ducked her head a little more so that Olena couldn't see the tears welling up in her eyes. "That's okay. I don't have anyone but you to tell my secrets to. But if you could do me a favor, tell M- Baron, thank you. Tell him that I've never... never felt so alive before, but it... *We* can't pretend that it's anything more than what we've already had."

How she managed a smile, she'd never know.

Her heart was breaking apart inside her chest.

Olena sat up in her chair and reached for her hand, but Mahina pulled her own hand away.

Instinct told her that Olena might not let go if she did.

Ninety-nine percent of her heart told her to let Olena grab a hold of her and let her hold tight, but that one percent, which was riddled in fear, told her that the man *helping* her mother would never let go of her.

And she'd failed her mother enough.

Sato wasn't the man he said he was. He was keeping secrets, too. Mahina knew that the secret Baron's unit had kept was for their safety.

Sato's were for selfish reasons. When she met him, she'd been desperate for help and dazzled by the man who seemed to have all of the answers.

Sato had money to burn and wanted to use it to take care of her mother. The whole situation seemed too good to be true.

And now she knew that it had been.

Her *little* talk with Sato had been anything but. He'd sat her down and explained their connection to each other and why they'd been kept apart. Seeing photos of his father... her *grandfather*, had left her stunned. The way that Sato had talked about him, made him almost godlike in some ways, but she just couldn't seem to feel that same emotion for the man.

If her grandfather had gone through so much effort to keep them away from his son. If he'd lied and plotted so much, she couldn't imagine revering him the way Sato seemed to.

Everything that he revealed to her was still struggling to sink in. After over an hour of talking at her, where he revealed his family's sordid past, only served to make one thing very clear.

She was the daughter of a criminal. One who admitted to targeting and hurting Olena and Cullen's military unit. He was even thrilled to let her know that they weren't just soldiers in the army. They were Delta Force operators as if his revelation would make her think badly of Malcolm.

That was far from the truth, but it had also cemented one thing in her head. She had to stay away from Malcolm. If Sato had no regret for trying to kill her friend, Mahina was under no misunderstanding that he might try again.

Or try to hurt more from Malcolm's team.

Mahina knew that she'd walked right into his trap.

And now, she couldn't get out.

Telling Olena would only bring her friend into the problems that she was facing, and he'd already kidnapped her friend and tried to end her life once before.

Mahina was going to do what she had to to protect the people in her life.

Even this lunch had been done for a purpose.

It was her chance to say goodbye. She would assure Olena that she was fine. Then she would promise to see her again, but that wouldn't happen.

That wasn't an option for herself.

Sato had played the role of generous benefactor, but he also threatened to play the role of cruel father.

What she'd seen in his eyes left no doubt that he could do exactly what he said. She would do what she could to protect the people she loved, and that would be her last gift to them.

They might never know that she was doing it to save them, but that didn't matter much. As she'd always been told, it's the thought that counts.

Mahina reached into her purse and pulled out two hundred dollar bills that Sato had given her.

She placed them on the tabletop and stood up from her chair.

"Wait." Olena reached out and wrapped her hand around Mahina's wrist. "Don't go. Not yet. I have some questions."

Mahina slowly pulled her arm free of Olena's grasp.

She gave her oldest and dearest friend a smile that she hoped looked as real as she could make it. "Stay, enjoy your meal. I'm going to head out and I'll call you later, okay?"

"Mahina, stop."

What little she held in her stomach threatened to come back up, but if she did that in front of her friend, she would know, without a doubt, that something was wrong.

Mahina had to find a way to make her friend let her go.

"Remember a long time ago when we were in grade school, that promise we made to each other?"

Olena smiled and the joy in it felt like Mahina had stabbed herself in the chest. "Of course I do."

"We promised each other that we could have one favor, at any time, any place, no questions asked."

As soon as she said the words, she saw Olena's whole expression fall.

"I remember."

Now Mahina could smile and mean it.

"Now I'm going to go and that's the end of that, okay?"

It took a moment, but Olena nodded once. "Okay."

That almost fixed the problem.

Almost.

Mahina knew that she wouldn't be able to make it back to the house before she lost the little bit of lunch that she'd managed to swallow.

She had to go to the ladies' room and splash some water on her face first.

With a quick wave, Mahina walked toward the back of the restaurant, struggling to remember if there was a door outside in that hall. She wanted to avoid walking past Olena if she could.

The last thing she wanted was for Olena to have another opportunity to stop her.

Mahina ducked through the half curtains that hung in the entry to the bathrooms and reached out a hand to push open the door.

A hand clamped over her mouth and an arm wrapped around her. A heartbeat later, she was pulled into the storage room with the door locked behind her.

NINETEEN

Mahina was frozen in fear until the light turned on overhead.

She didn't see one of Sato's security guards, it was-

"Mal!"

His gaze moved over her face and his hands, well, his hands were on her arms, her back, her hips and then he yanked her against his body.

Colliding with him was like stumbling into a wall.

But walls couldn't kiss.

And Malcolm was kissing her, his tongue sliding against hers in the most deliciously aggressive way.

All she could do was hang on, her arms wrapping around him, her knees going weak.

But he had her well in hand.

He held her up.

And he made her heart pound in her chest.

SHE WAS thunder and lightning in his arms.

She fit against him in all the right places, and when she

opened her mouth to him, he wished that he'd taken her straight out to his Jeep instead of the storeroom.

He wanted to fall into her soul and never come back out again.

He pulled away and looked down into her gorgeous dark brown eyes. "I'm sorry."

She blinked back at him. "What?"

"I said," he gave her another kiss before tearing his mouth away from her, "I'm sorry."

He watched a silent laugh play across her features.

"What?"

Her eyes narrowed at him. "I don't know why you'd say that. You haven't done anything."

"I left you. At the hospital. I should have gone back. I should have-"

"It's better that way."

He drew up short at her words.

They were softly spoken, but she didn't hesitate.

"*Hina,* I-"

"Baron." She put her hands between them, palms against his chest, and she stepped back, using her arms to put distance between them. "I need to go."

He heard her, but he didn't want to listen.

"I'll go with you."

She smiled, but it didn't quite look right. It looked strained. So wrong. "You can't."

"Yes," he stepped toward her, and she backed up. He kept walking until she had her back against the wall, "I can." Baron braced his hands against the wall beside her head, caging her in.

She still had plenty of room to move.

She could easily duck under his arm and walk away, but he hoped to keep her there long enough to talk.

"I don't want to argue with you." Her lips pressed into a

thin line and her chin trembled. "And I need to go."

She ducked under his arm and reached for the door.

All of his good intentions went right out the window.

With one step, he put his hand on the door and his muscular form meant that he had the weight and the speed to close it before she could get out.

Mahina leaned her forehead against the door, and he lowered his hand to her shoulder.

"What's wrong?"

"Nothing."

He could barely hear her. "I can't fix it if I don't know what I did."

"Why do you think *you* did anything?" Her voice was thinner, higher. "It's not something you did. It's me. It's my life."

Baron had his hands on her shoulders, trying to turn her around so he could look her in the eye, but she wouldn't budge. One look told him that she still had her hand on the doorknob.

He would, probably for the first time in his life, have to rely on words.

"And what about your life means that you need to leave? What says I can't go with you?"

He had her caught with his words. He was sure of it.

He had more staying power when it came to arguing. He was more stubborn, a trait he didn't think was very helpful until she tried to walk out on him.

"You can't tell me, can you? You can't put it into words and that's why I think you don't believe what you're saying. Sure," he leaned in a little more, lowering his hands to the point just above her elbows and gently held her arms, "you can tell me I didn't do anything, but is that the truth? If I've done something wrong, can you give me a chance to fix it?"

She hadn't said a word. She hadn't even moved.

"I've been a complete ass without you. My whole team

was ready to kick my ass unless I told them what was really bothering me.

"But they knew what it was. I didn't even have to tell them. And they knew that I needed to pull my head out of my ass before I could begin to fix it.

"So here I am. Here I am skulking in a back hallway, hoping to see you. And if you went out the front, I was close enough to run after you in the parking lot."

Again, he tried to turn her around, but she leaned into the door, her body tense and stiff.

The room they were standing in had shelves on two sides, left and right of the door, but like most storerooms it didn't have windows.

With their weight on the door and the single bulb above their heads, the room was very small indeed.

And the heat of her body near his wasn't something he could ignore.

He lowered his head and put his cheek against hers.

For a moment, she turned to him, rubbed her soft skin against the scratch of his.

But that lasted just a moment and she turned her head to the other side.

He wanted to pull the door off of its hinges just to make her turn and face him, but he didn't want her to turn toward him in fear. He might be an asshole, but he wasn't a man to use violence against a woman.

So how could he get her to look at him?

Talk to him?

His hands moved down her arms and when they reached her fingertips, he folded their fingers together and leaned in, placing a kiss against the side of her neck.

He felt her shiver this time, instead of pulling away.

Having her body respond to him when her mind had shut him out was perhaps the only way to reach her.

Thankful for the wide-necked blouse that she wore, he trailed his lips across her skin, making use of every inch that he could find.

Her breathing changed. Shallower. Faster.

He wanted her breathless.

He crowded closer, meaning only to bring himself close enough to feel her heat against him... there. But he stepped too close and brought himself flush against her.

At first, she pushed back into him, but before he could relish the touch of her softness against his cock, she pulled back, moving closer to the door.

If he'd had more control, he would have kept silent.

Should have.

"Don't you want me anymore?"

The question seemed to break them both.

A soft, sobbing cry came from her lips. "Of course I want you."

Then everything was fine.

He could handle anything as long as she wanted him. He could work with sex. He could work with lust.

He could get her to love him.

She shifted against him, putting her hands on the flat surface of the door and pushed back.

His eyes shut in bliss as her warmth cradled his iron hard erection.

"You're going to kill me like this."

She was crying and when he tried to pull back and give her space, her hand reached back and grabbed a hold of the back of his thigh.

"Don't." She swallowed, and the sound was more of a hiccup. "Don't pull away. I need this." Her fingers dug into the back of his thigh, biting in. "I need you."

Well, fuck.

There wasn't a power in the entire world that could have pulled him away after that.

He certainly wasn't going to deny her.

One hand lifted the back of her skirt and the other reached under. Together, they pulled down her panties and when she moved her feet, the cotton slipped down her thighs. He reached for his pocket and realized he hadn't brought anything with him. "Hina, I-"

"I'm on the pill. Don't make me wait."

And he wasn't. He didn't want her to change her mind.

He pulled down the zipper of his jeans and fuck, he heard her whimper.

"Turn around, Hina. Let me see your eyes."

She shook her head and bowed it forward.

He wasn't going to argue with her. Not when he could smell her perfume mixed with the heat of her arousal.

He was going to go nuts if he didn't have her soon.

She seemed to be feeling the same way.

"Hold still for a moment, baby. If you move, I don't think I'll be able to hold back."

"What if-"

He slipped a hand around to the front of her thigh and between her legs.

"Oh god."

And with his other hand wrapped around the base of his cock, he moved it against her.

"Mal..."

He smiled, or rather, his teeth gnashed together at the sound of his name on her lips. Fuck, he wanted to make her scream it.

It might have been a nightmare, the tight space, her frantic movements, his aching cock, but instead it was just perfect.

His hand between her legs helped guide her, helped open

her legs and her slick folds. And his chest against her back, bent her forward enough that he fit himself into her body like they'd been lovers for years.

He was inside of her in one deep thrust, and her body shuddered between him and the door.

Buried inside of her, he flattened a hand against the wall and used his other hand to tease her clit.

It didn't take long for the two of them to find the right angle, the right rhythm between them. There was just something so right about making love to her. Baron didn't know how he'd be able to let her go.

She wanted him to. She'd made that clear, but he couldn't.

Why, when this was so good, did she want him to stay away from her?

He pushed the thoughts aside to concentrate on her, always her. What else could he do but lose himself in her? Something he knew he needed for the rest of his life.

But this encounter was over in minutes, her body constricting around his, pulling a soft string of curses from his lips and the thick ropes of his orgasm from his body. He had to hold her around her waist and against his chest to keep them both from staggering and falling to the ground, exhausted and spent.

When she smoothed her clothes down, pushing his hands away from her body, he didn't fight.

When she reached down to the floor and picked up her discarded underwear, she put it into her bag and reached for the doorknob.

She held herself still for a moment and he took one more chance to speak to her.

"Stay, Mahina. Talk. Tell me what I need to do to keep us together."

Her chin dropped and she stared at the floor between them. "You're not the problem, Mal. Malcolm." He saw the tension tightening her shoulders. "I can't be with you. Not even like this. Never again. Please," she turned her head slightly to the side and looked at him, her eyes shining bright with tears, "if you care for me at all, just stay away. It'll be better this way."

He backed up, righting his own clothes as she tugged the door open. The light from the hallway flooded in as she darted outside.

He gave her to the count of three and then he followed her outside, determined to do exactly what he said he'd do, fix it.

TWENTY

When she returned to the house, the door opened, and Sato stood there. He stared at her for a long moment before his eyes narrowed and he opened his mouth to speak.

"Don't." She shook her head and tried to ignore the flash of anger she saw there. "I did what you wanted. I saw Olena. I lied right to her face when I told her I'd call."

As she passed him in the doorway, she held out her phone.

He reached for it, but the moment before he closed his fingers around it, she sent it crashing to the floor.

"Stop!" He gripped her arm and swung her around to face him. "That was unnecessary."

"Perhaps to you, it was." She glared at him. "Now, if you want information from my phone. You'll have to work for it. I've followed your orders enough today. I need to see my mother."

"You forget," his syllables were clipped and clean, "I am your father."

"How could I?" She tried to pull in a breath, but it stuck in her throat. "You seem to think that it entitles you to dictate my life. You make demands and I'm stuck here, making you happy. I wouldn't be surprised if you were the reason that I lost my job."

He was silent for a moment too long, and she felt her heart constrict in her chest.

"How?"

"I have many connections, Mahina. Your job was funded through my donation. It shouldn't surprise you if I take it away as well."

"How long?" She blinked back tears. "How long have you been pulling strings in my life?"

His casual shrug felt like a slap across her cheek. "Just before Suzume started her decline."

She drew back from him. "Did you..."

"Did I what?" He walked closer, his shoulders tense, his hands balled into fists.

"Did you make her sick, too?"

She saw it coming as if it was in slow motion, but she didn't even try to avoid the slap.

The pain was welcome and matched the horrible ache in her chest where her heart had been.

The slap affected Sato as well.

He seemed horrified at the action, staring at his hand and then at her face, he couldn't seem to believe what he had done.

Mahina felt the sting as if it was a hot iron that had touched her face.

"You'll learn, Mahina. You'll learn who I am."

She stared him right in the eye and hoped that he might see in her gaze what she wouldn't dare say in words.

She had already learned who he was.

And she didn't like it.

She hated it.

Hated him.

Lifting her hand to her cheek, she knew she'd need to see her mother, but she had to try and hide the mark that he'd left on her face. Mahina turned to leave.

"You should be careful, *daughter*."

Mahina needed a breath before she turned back to look at him. She was on the edge and afraid that she might act out. "Careful? Why?"

"There are always consequences for our actions."

Oh, that was rich.

"I know that." She tried to keep her emotions calm, but it wasn't possible. Her whole world had been turned upside down. "I've turned my back on my best friend and her family, which has been our family all of my life. All of the friends that I've managed to make. I think I understand consequences." She willed herself to stop talking, but it just didn't seem like she could stop. "If it wasn't for my mother and the care she needs, I would have walked away from you the day you decided to tell me who you were."

With that, she walked toward her room, which was more like a cell than anything else.

"Mahina."

She kept walking.

"Mahina!"

If he struck her down right then and there she might consider it a favor. There was only one thing left in her life that she loved. She would stay for her mother, but if something ever happened to her...

BARON LOOKED at the picture on his phone and narrowed his eyes. There was something familiar about the image.

Something that bothered him on an elemental level. He just couldn't put a finger on it.

He called Olena and while he waited for her to pick up the call, he sent the picture he'd just taken.

The call picked up a couple of rings later.

"Where did you take that?"

"Where? I followed Mahina back to-"

"It's him."

There was something about the tremor in Olena's voice that had Baron on alert.

"It's him." Her voice was barely a whisper. "I thought I'd never see him again."

Her voice was so thin, he wasn't sure he was hearing her correctly.

"Baron? This is Cullen. You're on speaker. What the fuck is going on?"

Baron felt his stomach twist inside of him.

"I followed Mahina from the restaurant at lunch. She went to a house in Kahala, and a man came out to talk to her when she got there."

The phone on the other side was silent.

Silent, except for Olena's frantic gasps for air.

"Fuck."

Cullen's voice was quiet, but crystal clear.

His friend was furious.

"It's the man who killed Mace."

Baron's blood ran cold.

He leaned over to the passenger seat and reached under it before he remembered that he didn't have his side arm back. "Fucking red tape."

"Baron? What's going on?" Cullen bit out his words. "What are you-"

"My handgun. HPD still has it. They've been dicking around with releasing it to me after that night at Kaena Point."

"Good."

Baron's ire flared at Cullen's words. "What the hell do you mean? Good? Fuck off!"

"If you had the gun," Cullen shot back, "what would you be doing right now?"

"I'd be inside that fucking house putting a bullet in his head."

"Yeah, good. You're too pissed off for this, man. Get your shit together and come over here. I'll call the others. We're going to get him, but we're going to do it right."

Right to Baron meant a bullet in the fucker's head.

That was it. A bullet and Mahina back home with him where she belonged.

But he had to admit that Cullen had a point.

He'd already pissed off some of the higher ups at the Honolulu Police Department. So far, he'd managed to keep himself out of jail by giving HPD full credit for the bust.

Credit he didn't fucking care about, so that was fine with him.

But yeah, if he'd had his gun back from the police, he'd already have gone in after Mahina.

Cullen was right, which Baron wouldn't admit to his friend.

Dropping his phone down on the passenger seat, he started the engine of his Commando and pulled away from the curb, heading to Olena's house.

SUZUME HEARD the yelling in the house, and it killed her.

The Sato that she remembered from years ago was long gone.

The sweet man who'd held her hand as they walked along at night, he'd died some time ago.

The man who had brought her flowers and showered her

with praise and attention the night that she had been crowned the Cherry Blossom Queen had disappeared into the wind.

And the man who'd shown her the only taste of passion that she'd experienced was now holding her daughter prisoner.

Mahina, the child she loved unconditionally.

The child who had suffered her mother's cold and caustic words during her illness? The child who had endured her mother's broken heart.

She was trapped in this house because she loved her mother.

Suzume knew that if she wasn't there. If she hadn't survived her illness and the septic infection that had nearly claimed her life, Mahina would never have made a deal with her father.

And now, they were both trapped.

What could she do?

A wind blew into her room from the ocean, bringing with it the scent of salt water and sea air.

It reminded her of long ago. Of Japan.

Her parents had brought her to Hawaii when they immigrated to America after the war, but they brought with them the old ways. The stories. The cultural ideas that were part of their homeland.

And it was those stories that rose up in her mind now.

She wished that she could wait and hope for more time to gain her strength, but the loud words from Sato to Mahina told her that frustrations were building.

Her daughter had done so much to care for her, she wanted to give something back.

To give Mahina her freedom.

Slowly, she began to move her legs and feet, hoping to increase the flow of blood into her limbs. It ached and it stung, but pain, she realized, meant that her circulation was increasing.

Staring out at the unending ocean, Suzume focused on gathering her strength so that she could act when she needed to.

HIS WHOLE TEAM converged on Olena and Cullen's home in less than an hour. Baron was barely able to control his anger and his need to act.

He couldn't say it out loud, but when Samira came in a moment after her husband, he was thankful for her presence.

Living just a few houses down from the commander on base at Schofield had done him good. Samira made her presence known and often invited him over for meals.

She seemed to understand his moods better than others, but rather than trying to get him to change, she gave him a chance to fret and fume in her calm and gentle presence, taking the edge off like setting a spoon over a pot of boiling water. She helped him settle himself.

And at the moment, he needed it, more than he could express.

She sat herself down beside him and touched his arm for a moment.

The simple gesture reminded him to breathe and took the edge off of his anger as Cullen took point in relaying the information that they'd discovered.

Boss was the only one of them who hadn't served with Mace, but his loss was still meaningful for him.

"Olena's father is at HPD Headquarters. They're organizing the tactical breach of the property."

Samira took his hand and held it tight, her gaze falling on his face.

"A warrant was drafted and waiting for a judge's signature before they can enter the property." Cullen's voice thickened. "I know we're all struggling with the idea of letting HPD take point here, but it's a civilian area and as far from a military property or installation as we can be on the island."

Olena lifted her head from where she had it pillowed on her knees. "As long as he's brought to justice, that's what we need to focus on. I know that I haven't forgotten what he took from us, but this can't be how we handle this."

"I should be there," Baron felt his words clawing out of his throat, "I was there already. I shouldn't have left."

Ajax stood, putting his hand on Hi'ilani's shoulder. "If we were here as Delta, I would have no problem leading all of you into the house, but don't have enough intel to make sure that we wouldn't be causing more of a problem than we'd be helping."

"I know it's wrong to say that I don't care." Baron barely kept himself in his seat. It if wasn't for Samira's hand gripping his, he would be in his Jeep, headed back to Kahala. "But I'd gladly take the man out on my own. Prison would be heaven as long as I know that she's safe."

Shado sat forward on the couch and met his gaze. "We know. Any one of us would, but you're also emotionally involved."

"Of course I am!"

Baron was ready to launch himself off of the chair, but it was his worry for Mahina and Olena's watchful eye that kept him in place.

MAHINA KNEW that she'd shut off any avenue of escape. "Stupid." She squeezed her eyes shut and pressed against her temples. "Stupid. Stupid. Stupid."

She hadn't just surrendered her phone.

She'd smashed it against the floor.

There was no way for her to know if it was still working and all of the other phones that had been in the house had been removed.

Her only possible avenue of escape was to leave the property and find her way to another house, but that meant leaving her mother alone with...

She just couldn't see him as a father.

Not hers.

Not for anyone.

Olena's dad had always been her dream of a father.

Busy, but always there for his kids.

Bent over the desk in her room, Mahina was drawing out the floor plan of the house, looking for ways that she might be able to get out of the house if the opportunity presented itself.

She was done with following the rules, but she wasn't going to be stupid about it.

She'd done enough of that.

Mahina just hoped that she would have a real chance at changing things.

TWENTY-ONE

It didn't take long for Olena's father to Skype in from the command vehicle as the SWAT team assembled to arrest Sato on a laundry list of charges. Everything from theft and drug charges on three islands, kidnapping and yes, murder. The fact that Mace had been a newly minted Honolulu Police Department officer added the enhancements of a 'cop killer' to the mix.

Everyone was fixed on the screen and listening to the SWAT team's plans for the takedown, absorbing every word and nuance when Ajax looked up and surveyed the group with a lightning quick eye.

"Where's Baron?"

Chairs emptied out as the team moved outside toward their vehicles.

The momentary relief that rushed through the group when they saw Baron's Jeep Commando in the driveway plummeted when they realized that Boss' truck was missing from the back of the group.

Boss pulled out his key ring and looked at the group. "We should've known."

Every single Delta nodded at the sentiment.

Baron had been the last of them to fall in love, but they'd often speculated that he'd go down hard and fast.

Now they just had to hope that he didn't let his passion cloud his judgement.

They couldn't lose another member of their family.

Ajax hit the nail on the head when he looked up and let his gaze fall on all of their team. "Let's go see how we can help the asshole."

It was that moment of levity that they needed to take the edge off of their worry. And as the commander climbed into Ajax's truck with him, he gave Jackson a subtle nod. "Baron couldn't have said it any better himself."

THE HEAT of the day was still oppressive as the sky changed from the bright glow of the afternoon to the jewel-like colors of sunset.

Suzume pushed her blanket off of her legs and turned her head toward the door. Her nurse had just finished with all of her vitals and while her energy had built up over the last few hours like a battery, Suzume had been quite the actress, feigning sleep and weakness.

She'd never been much of an actress, but she could lounge and stare with the best of them. While she'd been ill, she had more than enough practice.

Now, she put that all behind her and used the remote to move the parts of the hospital bed so that she could step down to the floor without the danger of injuring herself.

That would only ruin her plan.

There was a door out to the backyard directly from her room and she used that door, enjoying the heat soaking into her feet from the stone steps. When she reached the grass,

Suzume took a moment to close her eyes and feel the wind kiss her skin.

After staying in bed for so long, her knees threatened to buckle, but the volcanic rock wall that ran along the edge of the property gave her a decent enough hand hold to stay on her feet.

And when her hands couldn't hold on, her hip would land against the rock and keep her standing.

She hissed as the jagged rock poked through the cotton of her gown and abraded her skin, but that pain wouldn't last long once she reached the water's edge.

There were transcendent things that would only matter a moment or two before the endless deep swallowed her whole. Those were the things that she could put aside because the only thought that mattered was her daughter.

As she reached the sand, Suzume felt the heat again and she stumbled as there was no longer a wall to hold her up. She cried out as she fell to her hands and knees, but she bit down on her lips to stifle the sound.

The closer she got to the water, her mind mulled over the old stories. The mothers who had been trapped by their husbands in loveless marriages. The men who had no duty to their families and fixed their minds on their own needs and pleasures. Those mothers left to despair and watch their children starve and suffer had chosen a way to save them from the pain.

The practice wasn't followed much anymore, falling into disuse like so many other beliefs as the world modernized. There were few that still spoke of such things outside of the country, but the betrayal that she'd suffered through was from another age. Sato certainly acted like he saw himself as a feudal lord who lived by the sword.

This was the only thing she could do to challenge his

control, but it would also free her daughter to run back to those who could protect her.

Suzume knew that she hadn't been able to protect her daughter in years.

The moment that the water coursed over her hands Suzume fought to stand on her feet.

It might not be an honorable end like it once was, but she would attempt to meet her end moving forward until the world dropped away under her feet.

MAHINA HAD A PLAN. She would talk to her mother and explain what she was determined to do.

She might have closed the door between herself and Malcolm, but she remembered something that Baron had once said to another one of his team as they bantered back and forth.

When Shado's friend on base had lost out on a promotion, Shado had explained the encouragement that he'd given the other man. "When one door closes, open a window."

Baron had scoffed at the idea. "When one door opens, turn the damn knob, that's how they work."

Her plan was to follow her diagram to keep out of sight and leave the property and call for help. Baron would help.

They might see him as a surly, asshole, but he had honor.

Something her father had lost over the years.

Later, she would suffer the consequences of her actions, but at least they would be free.

Tucking the paper and her pen into the deepest recesses of her pants pocket, she moved to the door and wrapped her hand around the knob.

Twisting her hand, she felt the metal slide against her skin but that was all.

The door was locked.

———

IF ANYONE COULD HELP him reach Mahina, it would be her mother. It might also give him a way to bridge the divide with Suzume if they were working together to better his relationship with their daughter.

Knowing that Mahina was stuck in her room, he would have the time he needed to talk to her mother. Reaching the door to Suzume's suite, Sato pushed open the door.

The bed was empty.

The back door open.

He looked out at the expansive backyard and searched for any sign of movement. Any disturbance.

Sato didn't see anything in the yard. Taking a few steps out onto the grass he saw her.

In the water, nearly up to her shoulders.

Suzume.

"Suzume!" He called out to her, and she turned her head to look at him.

The look in her eyes was haunted.

Ghostly.

"Obake." The word whispered past his lips and disappeared on the wind.

What could he do at that moment?

A cold fist of fear closed around his heart.

He remembered the stories from Japan, the desperate actions of mothers with broken hearts.

Could she have taken Mahina into the water?

Would she try to take their child with her?

Given the choice between one or the other, Sato ran inside, fishing his keys from his pocket.

BARON KNEW that he'd arrived before SWAT.

The texts he'd received from his team told him so in a roundabout way. Telling him to stay out of the way when the SWAT team arrived.

And he would.

He had no interest in killing anyone. He couldn't shoot them unless he managed to get his hands on a weapon at the house.

He had one simple goal.

Get to Mahina and keep her safe.

Once he had his eyes on her and his arms around her, everything else was secondary.

There was a beach access near the home that might take a few minutes to find. It wasn't easy to find for a reason.

Local residents didn't want tourists wandering about in Kahala. The houses there were some of the higher priced homes in the area. They wouldn't want just anyone on their beaches.

Their access lanes had become mere walkways with the use of wild greenery and clever landscaping. He knew just what to look for. You didn't train to track through all kinds of terrain without learning what an overgrown path looked like.

He jammed on the breaks between two ornate brass gates, directly in front of a fire hydrant.

He knew how illegal that was, but he'd pay Boss for any tickets or damage he incurred.

Baron had to get inside the property immediately.

He hit the ground running, pushing palm fronds and lilikoi vines aside with his forearms and kept going until he saw the brilliantly colored sky over his head.

Sunset.

Time was running out.

DURING THEIR AFTER-WORK practice along the coast, the Maunalani Canoe Club had just turned back around under the Diamond Head Lighthouse when the stroker at the lead of the canoe caught sight of something in the water.

Pulling their paddle from the water they turned to look at the rest of the crew. "There's someone in the water!"

The steersman at the back of the canoe caught sight of a body in the water and turned the outrigger in its direction.

They had no way of knowing if they were going to perform a rescue or a recovery. They all hoped for rescue.

TWENTY-TWO

The door opened as Mahina was trying to pry open the window. The lamp base that she was holding slipped in her hands.

She caught it up and adjusted her hold on it, her gaze fixed on his, daring him to do or say something.

"You want out, Mahina?"

She turned her head a little to the side, wondering what his game was.

He turned as well, moving out of the doorway. "There you go."

Mahina rocked forward and then back again on the bottoms of her feet. She was poised to run, but she was wondering where.

Her father might be older than her, but she had a feeling that he was in good shape. When he'd outlined his crimes to her, he'd seem pleased and proud of the pain and suffering that he'd caused.

Why wouldn't it extend to her?

"I'm waiting."

His tone was silvery, his expression mild, and even

though she knew she might regret it, she figured that OUT was better than IN.

She walked past him and continued out into the hallway.

As soon as she saw his shadow closing in on hers on the marble tiled floor, she took off running.

———

HE WAS in the backyard before he realized it and he saw three men running off down the beach in their black suitcoats.

Bodyguards on the run.

What they were running from, he didn't know.

Didn't care.

If Olena's dad was right, there were likely men or women on the take within the HPD. Had they found out about the raid and the warrant?

It could be anyone with information in the judiciary, too.

Clerks, judges, hell, even a well-placed secretary could deliver the information needed.

He turned back toward the house and stopped short.

Sato dragged Mahina down the shallow steps into the backyard, his hold on her arm looked painful, but it was the expression on her face as they saw the empty room on the far side of the house.

She wrenched her arm from his and pointed at the open door. "Where is she?"

"Stop!"

"Freeze!"

Baron turned around and saw the men in suits being forced down into the sand face first, surrounded by SWAT officers.

Around the other side of the property, more SWAT officers came around the wall, their guns trained forward and their feet advancing across the grass.

"We have a warrant for your arrest! Get down on your knees! Interlock your fingers behind your head!"

Baron saw Mahina's face change from anger, to confusion, and then to horror as Sato reached out a hand and pulled her against him.

THROUGHOUT HER LIFE, Mahina had always read books. Books of any size. Any genre. All over the library shelves. And she'd read about characters who saw their lives flash before them right before they died.

When her father pulled her in and forced her to stand in front of him, using her as a kind of human shield, she didn't see her whole life flash before her eyes.

She saw the future that she would never have staring her right in the face.

Baron.

Malcolm.

"Mal."

"Mahina. Stay still."

How could she do any different?

Her father had a hand around her neck. A gun to her head.

It wasn't that she didn't want to move, she couldn't.

She wanted to live.

She just wasn't sure that she was going to get the chance.

"Sir! Let the woman go."

She looked out at the beach, following the voice and saw SWAT officers approaching on that side.

"Drop the gun down into the grass and get down on your knees!"

The men on the other side walked up along the edge of the pool.

She didn't know what to do.

She certainly had nothing to say.

All she could do was turn her gaze to the front and fix it on Baron.

"Mal," she corrected herself.

"That's right, Hina. Look at me. Right here."

He pointed at his face, and she was happy to do exactly what he said.

If something happened...

If her life were to end right at that very moment, she would take his memory with her.

"Daughter?"

A chill ran up her spine at the sound of his voice.

She had heard her father's voice communicate any number of scary emotions with it, but until that moment, she hadn't heard despair.

"There are many crimes that I've perpetrated in this world. I have stolen from many. I have addicted more than that. And I have killed. The only moment that I've ever regretted was this one."

She had no idea what he meant, but there was no time to ask.

She heard the click of the gun's hammer locking into place, and she knew she was going to die.

Mahina tried to lift her hands to hide the horror from Mal's eyes, but the explosion of a bullet from the barrel shook her and dropped her to the ground.

THE FLASH of the gun's muzzle would give him nightmares for years to come, but when he dove to the ground, reaching for Mahina, the face he held in his hands was pale but whole.

Her expression was a mixture of shock and confusion, but she was whole.

Malcolm Roth had never felt such abject fear coursing through his veins as he did in that moment, but the shock wore off faster for him than her.

He peeled off his shirt and used it to wipe blood off of her face.

When she lifted her hands to feel her hair, he pulled them away and brought her up against his chest, holding her tight.

As Mahina sobbed into his chest, he swore that he'd never let anything ever happen to her ever again, but he knew that he didn't have that kind of control.

No, Mahina had that kind of control over him.

The woman whose arms were close to squeezing the breath right of out of him had brought him to life in ways that he couldn't even begin to articulate, but he was going to spend the rest of his life trying.

Thanks to Olena and her father, he was able to take her inside and have her shower to wash off the evidence of her father's... sacrifice.

Baron had her close her eyes as he washed her from head to toe. He didn't want her to see the blood that coursed off of her skin and slipped down the drain.

He would always try to keep the horrors of the world from her. He knew that he couldn't guarantee success, but that didn't mean that he would stop trying.

A man like him might never stop being an asshole, but he'd die trying... for her.

OLENA APPEARED at her side wearing her own body armor and gear.

"Hey, thank god you're okay."

Mahina's eyes clouded over with tears. "I don't care about me. I need to find my mom. She wasn't in her room." Turning to look at the SWAT officers, she searched the crowd. "Can you ask them-"

"No need to ask." Olena gave her a bright smile. "Your mother was kind of crazy ingenious."

"What?"

Olena pulled out her phone and opened her text messages. Tapping on a photo she pinched her fingers over the photo and drew it out to show the image in full on the screen. "Look."

Mahina reached for the phone and almost dropped it.

"Careful there." Baron helped her steady her hands as she apologized to Olena.

"My hands are still shaking."

When she looked down at the image, she gasped in a breath. "Where... where is she?"

Baron leaned over her shoulder and Mahina held up the phone so he could see her mother sitting amongst a group of paddlers on the beach.

Olena tapped the top of the phone. "Apparently, your mom ventured out into the water to get away. She told the paddlers she didn't want your dad to use her to keep you in the house."

"But," Mahina shook her head, "but my mom doesn't swim."

Reality crashed in on her as her hands clutched the phone.

"My mom... she was going to-"

"Hey," Mahina heard Olena's voice as if it was from a mile away, "hey... look at me."

"She can't swim, Olena. She can't-"

"Look at me."

Mahina heard the words but couldn't seem to make her body follow.

"Look. At. Me."

Mahina's head snapped up and she looked into her friend's dark eyes.

"Maybe that's what she tried to do, but she didn't succeed, okay? And that's what we're going to do, Mahina. We're going to make sure that both of you are okay. Do you hear me?"

Nodding, Mahina fell into her friend's arms and held her as tight as the Kevlar vest allowed.

"Will you forgive me?" "Will you forgive me?"

Olena laughed and leaned in to kiss Mahina, one cheek and then the other. "If we're going to keep talking over each other, we're going to be in trouble."

"No."

Mahina turned and saw Cullen standing beside them, wrapping his arm around Olena's armor-broadened shoulders.

"We're the ones in trouble if you two can't stop talking over each other."

Olena elbowed Cullen in his gut and gave him a hard look. "Watch it, buddy. I know where you're ticklish."

Mahina felt Baron's arms tighten around her body as he leaned closer to Olena and Cullen.

"He's ticklish?"

Mahina started to laugh, her shoulders shaking until her eyes narrowed so she couldn't see. Baron turned her around in his arms and drew her against him. She knew that she was going to be really and truly okay when he started to laugh with her.

EPILOGUE

A few months later, the whole team took a trip to Las Vegas for Boss and Tehani's wedding. With his family and hers splitting the difference, everyone agreed to visit the Ninth Hawaiian Island and see the nuptials performed at The Little Church of the West.

Baron knew that there was going to be a bunch of events with people outside of his family. Tehani's family from Tahiti and Hawaii, and Devon's family from the Midwest. He managed not to put a grimace on his face, even with all of the extra people around him.

Looking at the woman sitting next to him at the rehearsal dinner, he knew why.

Even when they were at certain events, like the bachelor/bachelorette parties, Baron was fine with the distance from Mahina, because he knew they'd be together soon.

He was, as Samira liked to call him, enamored.

Baron rolled his eyes and winced as Mahina nudged him with her elbow. "What was that for?"

She leaned into his side and wrapped his arm around her shoulders.

"What are you rolling your eyes about?"

He shook his head and leaned in to press a kiss on her nose and then her lips. When he pulled back an inch, he smiled at her. "I was just remembering what Samira told me I am around you."

Mahina narrowed her eyes at him, but he saw the smile on her lips. "She called you hot? Sexy? Do I need to talk to her and tell her to back off my man?"

"No," he sighed, "you don't have to do that."

"Good," she nodded as the waiter brought more iced tea to fill her cup. "I like her too much to wrestle her over a guy."

His chin dropped to his chest, and he chuckled. "You're killing me."

"Killing you?" She took a drink from her cup and set it back down again. "How am I doing that?"

He leaned in and whispered in her ear. "You make me want to take you back to our room and make you scream my name."

He saw the heat that spread across her cheeks, but he also saw the quirky grin that lifted her lips.

When she spoke, he knew he was done for.

"So you mean a normal night for us?"

Leaning in again, he nipped at her earlobe and heard her hiss. "I'm going to have to put in some extra effort then."

She leaned away from him and narrowed her eyes. "Maybe not tonight. The wedding is tomorrow, and I need to walk down the aisle with you and the other girls. I won't look good if I'm having trouble walking."

He smiled and the look she gave him said she was imagining it. "Knowing my guys," he laughed under his breath, "all the women are going to be walking a little funny tomorrow."

"Well," she gave him a little side-eye look, "that sounds like a challenge I'm willing to sacrifice myself for."

She raised an eyebrow, and her smile tightened a little into a smirk.

Sitting beside her in the restaurant, he was suddenly very hard.

"Sacrifice for?" He felt his chest tighten. "Are you planning to let me have my way with you?"

Her breathing changed and her eyes darkened as he looked down into her eyes.

"Is it wrong that I think I'm full?" She moved her plate an inch or two in toward the center of the table. "Do you want to go back to our room?"

"Back to our room?" Baron shrugged his shoulders. "I guess so. You... want to lay down for a little while?"

"That is one option," she leaned in and whispered into his ear, "like if you want to be on top, or let me do that."

"I like those options." He had to lean a little in one direction to keep his slacks from choking off the blood flow to his dick. "I have a few more options if you're interested."

Mahina stood up, her chair scraping back a little, loud enough to turn a few heads at the table.

His gorgeous woman lifted a hand to cover her face and Baron loved it. Alone with him she could be a wild woman. Her confident nature kept him on his toes. In public or in a group of people she was still her amazing self, but she just wasn't as assertive as she was in his arms.

God, he loved her so damn much.

Baron got up and put his hands on her shoulders, standing behind her so that he didn't give everyone an eyeful, he looked at his friends. "We're kind of full."

Boss' shoulders shook. "Right. Full of it."

Tehani gave his shoulder a playful smack. "Be nice."

"Nice?" Shado almost choked on a bite of steak and Lilinoe rolled her eyes beside him. "Since when are any of us nice?"

Train gestured at the commander a few seats down. "He's the boy scout of the group."

"Uh," Olena rolled her eyes at Train, "there are at least three Eagle Scouts here at the table."

Samira pointed at Ajax, Cullen, and her husband. "That's three. But don't forget Baron."

Now it was Boss' chance to choke on a bite of food. "The asshole is an Eagle Scout?"

Baron laughed out loud. "I had to earn my merit badges like everyone else, but my Scout Master quit when I became Troop Leader. He said his heart couldn't take it."

He leaned in and placed a kiss on Mahina's temple. "So now that you know my sordid past as a Boy Scout, I'm taking my woman upstairs to our room."

Tehani waved at Mahina. "I'll see you tomorrow in our suite to get dressed for the ceremony."

Boss draped his arm over Tehani's shoulders. "We're meeting in Shado's room to put on our suits. Don't be late, asshole."

Mahina turned around and then turned him around as she waved over her shoulder. "See you all tomorrow!"

They heard the whole group calling after them as they walked away.

As soon as they cleared the front door of the restaurant, Mahina turned around and glared at him. The glare almost lasted more than a few heartbeats.

"Why do you two go after each other like that?"

Baron shrugged. "Habit?"

She rolled her eyes at him. "You and Boss think it's funny, but the restaurant manager was about to have a heart attack. He was standing along the wall with his hand over his heart.

That's why I got us both out of there. I was afraid that he was going to call the police."

"I doubt he would have done that, but I'm glad you got us out of that." He looked down at his watch before looking back at her with a big smile on his face. "If you hadn't, I would have had to figure out a way to do it."

Mahina laughed at him. "Are you that eager to get me up to the room?"

He pulled her close and hugged her. "You know it, Hina." Then he stepped back and took her hand in his. "Let's take a walk first. I got us a private event here in the hotel."

"Oh?" She walked along beside him, looking at him from time to time.

She didn't have to worry about walking into anything or anyone. She knew that Baron would keep her safe. So, when they stopped at an ornate set of glass doors, she had to look around to find a sign.

A big one beside the door told her that they were at the Bellagio Conservatory.

That, and the fact that they were closed.

"Baron?"

He gave her a pointed stare and she blushed.

"Malcolm?"

"That's better."

He leaned closer to the door and knocked on the glass with a soft rap of his knuckles.

The door opened and Mahina was surprised to see the interior lit with candlelight.

The man inside the conservatory gave Baron a nod. "You're good for an hour or so."

"Thanks, Joe." He put out his hand and tipped the man before they shook hands and Joe stepped out.

Baron walked her around the room, letting her enjoy the

beauty of the displays. Whenever she looked in his direction, she found him watching her.

"Aren't you going to enjoy the conservatory? The art... the flowers... it's all beautiful."

He grinned at her, his hand warming hers as he turned her to face him. "I'm enjoying the view just fine."

The look in his eyes was just as magical as the room they were standing in. The tree over their heads was decorated with colored glass lights hanging from the branches. "This room is incredible! How did you get us in to see it?"

The smile on his face said it was a bit of a secret and really, she didn't care. She was just amazed at what he'd arranged for them.

"Not bad for an asshole, right?"

The look she gave him was one that he probably expected. "When are you going to stop with that?"

He shrugged. "It doesn't bother me."

She slipped her arms under his and wrapped her arms around him. "I just don't want you to believe that about yourself. And I'm not all that enthused about the guys saying it to you."

She was sure that Baron thought she was a little silly for saying that, but it was the truth.

"You've gone all snarly, mama bear on me."

She looked up at him, frowning a little. Playfully.

"Nothing wrong with me getting protective of my man, right?"

"No." He leaned in and kissed her, nearly stealing her breath before he leaned back. "Nothing wrong with you being protective. I love it when you get like that. I love it when you get cuddly and run your hands all over me. And-"

She frowned a little when he reached behind his back and took her hands.

As he brought her hands around to his front, he continued to speak.

"I love you all the damn time, baby. I love you like crazy."

She felt her heart welling up with love inside of her.

He looked up into the tree above them and reached an arm up toward one of the branches.

As she watched, he tugged on a silver ribbon tied to one of the branches.

When he had it down, he held it in his hand and gave her a smile that she'd never seen before.

"Now, don't think I'm going to be this normal all of the time, but-"

Baron got down on one knee, held his hand out and opened his fingers so she could see the silver ribbon laid across his palm.

"I'm hoping you don't mind making an honest man out of me."

She blinked back tears. "You're always an honest man."

He smiled and she smiled before they both started to laugh.

"Then maybe you'll marry me and keep me in line... from time to time."

"And you'll push me over the line... from time to time."

Baron's eyes fixed on her face, and she felt her body heat up under his gaze. "And bend you over a few things. Whatever it takes to make you happy, Hina."

She felt tears rolling down her cheeks and lifted a hand to wipe them away.

He turned his head to the side and watched her as if she was a bomb about to explode. "So, is that a, yes?"

"Yes!" She clapped her hands over her mouth at the echo in the conservatory. "Oh my god, do you think someone heard that?"

Baron got up and kissed her like he wanted to breathe her in. "Ask me if I care. I'm getting fucking married."

He took her hand in his and slipped the engagement ring on her finger.

When he looked up into her eyes again, he spoke in almost a whisper.

"We're getting married."

Mahina nodded and lifted her hands to his face, drawing him down toward her lips. "Yes," she brushed a kiss across his lips, "we're getting married."

GLOSSARY

Hawaiian Word Pronunciation Guide

Twelve Letters in the Hawaiian Alphabet: 5 vowels (a, e, i, o, u) and 7 consonants (h, k, l, m, n, p, w)

Pronouncing the Vowels

A = AH

E = EH

I = EE

O = OH

U = OO

And because the Hawaiian language was purely verbal until the arrival of the Missionaries in Hawaii, no letter is ever silent. It is a purely phonetical language.

Below, you'll may find Hawaiian words, Japanese words, local/Pidgin English words and more

Words and Their Meanings (alphabetical order)

E kala mai ia'u - Forgive me

Gyotaku - a local Japanese Teishoku restaurant

- the artform of printing fish and sea creatures

Hanafura - a Japanese Card Game - matching sets based on nature (flora/fauna/etc)

Hanasu - A shorter, terse form of the verb 'Speak'

Kanaka or Kama'aina - Locals of Hawaii

Maika'i - okay

Makai - Water/Ocean side (direction)

Mauka - Mountain side (direction)

Nani - What in Japanese

Obake - ghost in Japanese - also a particular kind of large, pale anthurium flower

Oyako shine - a traditional form of suicide committed by mothers

Poke - typically an uncooked/raw chopped fish/seafood dish, flavored with oils, seaweed, nuts, etc

Zabuton - a large, square cushion for use on the floor

-floor seating in a traditional Japanese home

ABOUT THE AUTHOR

Reina reads like she writes:
  Heat to Sweet
  Contemporary to Historical
  Paranormal to well… Normal
  Military,
  First Responders,
  & More

Always with an HEA because we all deserve it!

Printed in Great Britain
by Amazon

36328542R00145